Spread the Wings:

Globalizing India

ARUP MITRA

WORDIT ART FUND

This book has been fully funded by the Wordit Art Fund. Wordit Art Fund
helps deserving authors publish their work by providing monetary
support. To apply for funding, please visit us at
www.BecomeShakespeare.com

First published in 2017 by

Becomeshakespeare.com
Wordit Content Design & Editing Services Pvt Ltd
Unit - 26, Building A-1, Nr Wadala RTO, Wadala (East),
Mumbai 400037, India
T:+91 8080226699

©
ISBN 978-93-86487-72-8

PREFACE

I0669520

In the backdrop of globalization and the changing ethos and value system it would be unreasonable to expect the Indian society to be an exception. In spite of the resilience observed in many segments there have been significant changes at least in certain layers. And these changes are no way less than what some of the developed countries are observing or have witnessed a couple of years back. A latecomer usually takes a quantum jump and to this the Indian society holds the biggest testimony, as the novel suggests.

Aruna, a scholar of history and art visits Paris and falls in love with two western guys, Philip and William, simultaneously. She experiences the somberness in Philip and adores it all along. On the other hand, the lustrous attraction of William is inescapable. Aruna does not want to bind her mind to one at the expense of another. She believes in leaving the heart unleashed so that the gems she gathers from the ocean of life are genuine. She realizes, both are indispensable and she cannot forego either. However, Aruna's passion for freedom is not selfish. She understands the compassion that Alice has for Philip and respects it sincerely. She does not want to posses Philip, depriving Alice, and thus motivates Philip not to choose one between herself and Alice, rather to accept both as time brings them in due course. Aruna also understands the bisexuality of William and accepts it full-heartedly. William's involvement with Dimitri does not inflict jealousy or rejection in her mind. She accepts the sexual bonding between the two young men. William also discovers that both Aruna and Dimitri are a part of his existence. With respect to one his longing is not complete - between the two one is not substitute for another. He, therefore, extends space to both without secrecy and hypocrisy.

The present legal system or the social norms are not adequate to give space to these accepted changes at the individual level. The notion of marriage in the legal framework is not compatible with the marriage of true minds that characters in the fiction find. Thus they do not bother to seek a legal acceptance of what they have chosen to be cohesive and comfortable. They are happy to work out their own equilibrium, and from the personal angle at least they feel, it works with stability.

The fiction also addresses a larger question concerning the definition of middle-class. The occupations, educational levels and the income levels which used to define middle-class quite coherently in the Indian context have changed so much so that the scholars now undertake full-fledged research exploring a more acceptable criterion. The present work through certain narrations tries to offer a lucid definition of this class to which Aruna belongs.

CONTENTS

Chapter 1

"Take the train from Saint Michel, in Porte de Clignancourt direction, and change at Chatelet", said the lady at the counter with a thick French ascent. "But that is in the opposite direction", said Aruna after scrutinizing the city map. "Well you get a connection there; sometimes to reach the right place you will have to go the wrong way", the lady gave a broad smile. "Or just walk along the river Seine and you would reach Louvre in about 10 to 15 minutes". Aruna thanked her and proceeded fast. The whole day she would spend in Louvre, she had decided. The statue of Venus, the paintings of da Vince, Bellini and many others and the mummy in deep sleep inside the glass box kept her mind captured. In addition, she spent considerable time in front of the images of Mercury and many other Roman and Greek gods, goddesses and the mythological stars, admiring the beauty of the curves the artists could bring out skillfully.

Aruna had studied history, archeology, art and comparative literature. A talented girl of twenty five had good command over her subjects and language as well. She looked at the paintings of the local artists outside the Louvre selling at a throw-away price for a livelihood. Even the world renowned artists whose paintings sell at an imaginary price today had to die of hunger. Who knows among the present ones also some may be worshipped by the future generation though his unfed skeletal body might have been reduced to mud by then somewhere in an ignoble corner of the earth. But that is how the human civilization has been. Few are lucky to receive recognition during their life-time. The photo of a person carries more weight than the living body. And that is because it is much easier to worship the past than the present. Many such thoughts crossed Aruna'a mind.

From the turmoil of the revolution against gross inequality there emerged a civilisation which believes in equality, liberty and fraternity. Aruna admired the tower of Bastille which was constructed to symbolize the revolution during which the prison of Bastille was demolished. Aruna kept watching the nude structure of the (male) angel of liberty upholding the torch in one hand and the broken chain in the other, with one toe on the earth and another feet in the air. "This is how liberty should be!" Aruna spoke to herself, "The wings are wide-opened. Perhaps India will also experience this liberty one day!" The freedom from poverty, social tyranny, superstitions and the new phenomenon of rising inequality with expressions of mindless consumerism! The social status depends on how much one is able to spend, making neighbours sleepless and questioning their own abilities and capabilities. Is this what India had imagined to experience at the onset of political freedom? Globalisation ushered in opportunities for those who already had plenty but not for those who had scanty. "How globalization can also be to the benefit of those who sleep in the street or live with inadequate basic necessities must be the concern of the political leaders, policy makers, social thinkers, the corporate world and the civil society", Aruna spoke to herself. Anyway, she thought, she was becoming too emotional. She again went back to the neighbourhood of Louvre from Bastille. She stepped into the gardens in front of the museum on her way back to her residence. She stopped for a while in front of the statue of a starving old-man holding his almost-lifeless sick son. With what sincerity the architect constructed this statue! The hungry looks, the sickness and the lifelessness are prominent – perhaps more expressive than the reality! Two drops of tears rolled down her cheeks unknowingly.

As the evening was drawing in Aruna felt a chill in the wind and decided to return to her hostel. She walked along the river and enjoyed the music the French youngsters were playing in groups. She thought, she could be a part of them. But an Indian hesitation stopped her from stretching her hands of friendship.

Aruna was in Paris on a scholarship from the French government for ten months. However, she did not mind staying longer. If luck favoured she might get an extension so that she would be able to complete her work before she returned to India. "Here the work atmosphere is so conducive whereas in India there is a great deal of activities with no output". Silence is more productive than words, she felt.

Chapter 2

Shyama is an Indian name given to a French lady. She had been a regular visitor to the Indian temple in the outskirts of Paris. Her association with the centre dates back to almost past twenty five years. Her son Philip was only five years old when she first came to meet some of the monks at the centre. Her husband was quite unwell and she was terribly disturbed. She needed some support to pass through the trauma and the centre did provide her a great deal of care. Since then she had been dedicated to the centre and kept offering social services.

The monks affectionately named her Shyama though she was as fair as a European. Philip a young man but like his mother had become a regular visitor to the centre. The monks named him Raghu. A tall handsome young man with bright eyes and a sharp nose Raghu bore a reserved personality. Spoke only when required otherwise preferred to observe silence. Not much expressions were evident in his face – mostly in a contemplative mood. Not much attention he paid to the external world when he was sitting next to the visitors though he did not make any mistake in performing his responsibilities he had been assigned to. He did not look into the eyes of too many visitors, smiled only gently, which was as rare as the moon-light at the edge of a patch of dark clouds. He listened to the conversations and added if anything was essential or asked for. From the young days spiritualism had bloomed in him like a lotus opening its petal one after another at the advent of morning light. Quietly he meditated and left the premises after everyone had retired to bed. At times he stayed back in the guest room spending hours together in deep meditation, sitting in the dark. He gazed at the stars – as if he was trying to track down the invisible traces of the wheels of the chariot moving from star to star in the depth of the night.

Philip's father had died ten years ago. Subsequently his mother had spent a couple of weeks with Philip at the centre. Philip took a strong liking to the somber atmosphere there. Whenever he went there he collected flowers from the garden, supervised the farm and helped process the agricultural produce. He always had a great deal of work awaiting him. The moment he entered the temple gate the Chief would scream in joy, "Oh the angel is here". Philip had already completed a course in agriculture technology. The temple had provided him a great deal of space and opportunities to convert his theoretical knowledge into practice. He was quite grateful to the monks for that rather than feeling exhausted.

Long ago when he was in school he had a girl friend. Both were quite fond of each other. But then one day he came to know that her parents had a major fight over some trivial issues and had decided to separate. The mother and daughter went away to Cyprus as the former got the job of a waitress in a restaurant. Philip missed her girl friend a great deal. And perhaps that was the time since when he started visiting the temple with his mother more frequently than before. Of late given his daily visits and long stay in the temple there was a rumor all around that he was going to be a monk soon. Of course the Chief would be more than delighted to accept him to the order. But then he had been asked to observe his own mind and assess the intensity of inclination. After all, it was not good to give up anything after accepting it with interest. Since it was a lifelong commitment one must take a decision carefully, both his mother and the Chief had explained to him.

Chapter 3

Someone told Aruna that she must visit India House if she did not want to miss her country in Paris. So one morning she decided to venture into that part of the city. In the metro station she met an Indian girl – a little younger than her – who was also going to the India house. The girl informed Aruna that there would be celebration of some festival which will be followed by cultural programme and lunch. Aruna was a bit surprised because she had known that the festival was long over. She had a chat over the last weekend with her sister over the phone and she had informed that all their uncles and aunts had come home in Jaipur for the festival. To settle Aruna's anxiety the Indian girl explained that the Indian festivals were usually observed abroad at the convenience of the participants – usually on a holiday – rather than going strictly by the dates. Aruna was pleased to receive the explanation.

After a few minutes of conversation and particularly after Aruna had introduced herself more than once she was naturally looking forward to knowing her companion's background. However, she felt that the other party was not forthcoming. This naturally enhanced a lady's curiosity. Aruna's questions became more probing though not very much yielding. Later she discovered that her companion was married several times in the past. Aruna was keen to know if that was her profession but then she learnt that it was all a harsh outcome of time and coincidences. Meena, as she revealed her name much later before getting down from the metro at Cite Universite, had married an old man first as she was keen to stay back in France. After pulling on for some time she fell in love with the old-man's son who had returned from USA. The son of course had thought that she was only a paying guest at his father's residence. The father one afternoon found both in the first floor room lying naked and right away went for a legal separation. The son was angry with her too for having kept everything in utter secrecy. She slept in the railway station for two nights after being driven away by the old man and then managed to pick up a guy from Tunisia. They lived together for a few months and then got married. The Tunisian man left her after sometime as he decided to migrate to Australia and Meena was reluctant to leave France. She had fallen in love with France though she could not manage to make a French man fall in love with her. After a long hunt she managed to find Tom. Of course she had a break-up with Tom a couple of months later because she found him too demanding. Then for the second time that they came together to give it a trial again. Obviously marriage had not taken place yet though she was very hopeful about it. All these stories Aruna heard from other Indians as soon as she reached the India house. "Gossip! Wherever we go we are the same!" said Aruna to herself. She consumed nothing of this sort and continued her friendship with Meena. She found her quite interesting though her head bore a thicker quoting of lice than hair. Much later when she visited her residence once, she found the thickness of dirt was too prominent to be covered by an embroidered bed-sheet. She met Tom as well. A young man who loved India quite intensely but was always trying to prove himself as macho, Aruna felt. "Why can't people be natural and spontaneous?" But the next moment she snubbed herself for being judgmental about others.

Chapter 4

At India House next to Aruna was sitting William, a young handsome guy with inexplicable beauty. Aruna had seen another guy, Philip a little while ago in the ground floor when he was entering with the Chief from the Indian temple, who had come to perform the worship at Indian house. The picture of Philip was creating a deep mark in Aruna's mind. She was retrospecting and hence, had not initially taken note of who was sitting next to her. Suddenly her eyes fell on this guy, William with a red shirt and an embroidered handkerchief tied around his neck. As he stood up to greet someone Aruna kept on watching his admirable physique.

Though not too tall he appeared as if an artist had carved him with admirable skill. Not an inch of extra flesh anywhere, a thin waist and a broad chest and shoulder drew many others' attention too. Some of the males kept staring at the slopes of his magnificent butt. The tight jeans suited him perfectly. "He must have worked on his abdomen and hip quite a lot", someone commented with an Indian ascent. Aruna quickly turned her eyes away as they met William's. The young man sat down again next to Aruna after completing his brief conversation with the entrants. There was a huge gathering at the auditorium to attend the cultural programme.

A little later Aruna saw Philip entering the hall and he came and stood almost next to where Aruna was sitting. Philip looked more complacent than when Aruna met him downstairs. Surely Philip too noticed Aruna but with his usual indifference he proceeded to the next row. Aruna remained spell-bound: "On the one hand beauty appears as smooth as the moon-beams, on the other it radiates like blooming spring, intoxicating all, irrespective of gender, age and status! Both the men are attractive, both stir the heart deeply and both keep the mind engrossed — yet there is somewhere a difference," Aruna reflected. Philip possessed a unique gravity. His eyes were half-closed, as if emerging from deep meditation. His grace was like the dark clouds of the July spreading over the sea-coast in India, just before the downpour. A tall guy with a prominent nose, blue eyes and a pair of thick brows did stand out sharply in the crowd. Each part of the body reflected discipline. "Discipline bears so much beauty and attraction! Yet, the movies have to display so much overflow and disquiet to attract the crowd," thought Aruna.

The festival was performed with great sincerity at the India house. It was such a pleasure to see people of different streams and countries joining the gathering. Their participation in the cultural programme was remarkable. With the moods and the lyrics the whistles and claps moved coherently. Some of the non-Indians were too prompt to pick up the origin of one or two popular number in Hindi. The music directors must be more careful not to expose the Indian habit of pursuing plagiarism so explicitly.

Aruna again got an opportunity to find both

the guys close to her. While distributing food Philip was there at the counter and with a broad smile he extended the plate to Aruna. She realized that he must have been a regular visitor to the India House and thus was entrusted with certain responsibilities. While talking to a couple of French girls Aruna's eyes fell on William, who was trying to converse with a group of Indian boys in Hindi. They were enjoying his accent. Aruna too laughed once or twice and William noticed it. He went for a second help and there he met Philip. Both greeted each other and Philip brought him some rice pudding and Indian sweets. William thanked him before leaving the counter.

Chapter 5

Aruna was walking along the bank of Siena. The waves emerged and stroke both sides of the river bank with every passing of the boats loaded with tourists. Aruna's mind had become like Siena. Philip had set in one set of waves while William another. They were not conflicting but they had captivated her mind. They were not similar either but both had captured her attention. They were distinct but impact-full in their own way. They were influencing her mind in two different manners, though. Aruna realized that she was getting attracted to both simultaneously. One was filling her empty heart like the clouds appearing in the sky after the summer months, making preparations for the downpour, and the parched up earth awaiting the rains to fill every crack and retain fertility. The other was filling her heart with a fragrance carried over by the intoxicating breeze - a youthful joy dancing around aimlessly - and within that fragrance there remained concealed the desire to bear and blossom.

Aruna quite aware of both the feelings in her, kept smiling to herself. She allowed them to raise their heads as much as they could. She knew, if one would start watching one's mind, though it is really difficult because in the process one tends to get merged with one's feelings, one would not get carried away by them. Either reasoning would prevail or one would get detached from the feelings after a while. Let time decide in due course.

Her mind was getting back again and again to William's red shirt matching perfectly his red lips and his proportionate and perfect physique with a sense of politeness in his eyes. After all, how devotionally he was sitting next to her with folded hands when the worship was going on! No one would dare to say, beauty and arrogance go together! When modesty resides in beauty, the latter looks more graceful and becomes more effective. And that was exactly what was happening at that point.

Even before the encounter at the food counter at India House Aruna suddenly recalled now while walking along the river that Philip had passed on some flowers to her when everyone was queuing up for the offerings. Aruna could not pave her way to the person who was distributing flowers. The crowd was too heavy. Philip with his long arms had got some extra and Aruna being his neighbour in the prayer hall had got the advantage. His wide eyes were appearing like two blue lotuses in the depth of her heart. She allowed them to appear as much as they could, and again went on walking along the track. She had reached Notre Dame, she realized.

The road was full of crowd — both tourists and residents. A clear sky slowly being approached by the dark cover of the evening, the purple twilight glittered like blue sapphire. Aruna tried to feel them deep down her very existence. She wanted to preserve every moment of her visit. After all, mind is a treasure house. Richer one gets by storing such rich experiences. Let not the space be filled with unnecessary ifs and buts or dos and don'ts. What is spontaneous has the originality and let that stay in its original form without any artificiality, without any fabrication in this store house. Aruna tried to recall some of his poems and kept reciting them to herself to match the situation and the mood. She took a turn then to reach Saint Michael. Stopped in front of a few stores for window sopping and then moved on. Saw some of the South Asians in the street but gone are the days when they used to give a sign of recognition when they met each other in the streets of foreign land. "Now with arrogance everyone turns away: as if it is a shame to be recognized, particularly by the peer group. Or possibly there are too many South Asians now in the streets of the western world and each one of them is bored of seeing the rest. Perhaps the talent required for being able to travel to the foreign land has declined now. With the emergence of the new rich class in India the connotation of worthiness has possibly changed drastically!" Aruna kept reflecting on the transformations that the world witnessed at a rapid pace. "Now many western people, who were known to be unfriendly unless you spoke their language, take the initiative to befriend you with their broken English", she thought.

Chapter 6

Quite unknowingly Aruna had started spending a great deal of time thinking about William, almost on a regular basis. His red shirt, wide eyes and his beautiful mouth all glittered like stars in the backdrop of his glamourous physique. Again, Aruna did not try to control her mind. She allowed it to move in its own way.

As she entered the metro-station at Cite, suddenly she saw someone she had been reflecting on. It was William! Wearing the same red shirt! In fact, Aruna was so surprised that she could not recognize him for a moment. She had been engrossed in her thoughts so much so that her inner eyes remained fixed on him and took no notice of the fact that her thoughts actually had become a reality. But William had recognized Aruna. How could Aruna tell him that she had been thinking about him all along and suddenly he appeared before her eyes! What a coincidence! Aruna felt shy and a unique hesitation held her tongue before she could proceed to say anything. She took a few seconds before she could respond to William.

"Aren't you the same girl sitting next to me yesterday at India House?" Asked William. "Yes", Aruna returned his greetings.

"So what are you up to? William enquired with a smile.

"Well nothing much, gathering facts and

figures relating to my work on history and art."

"Great! Lourvre is a treasure house for you."

"For all", Aruna replied gently. "Even for those who do not understand much the technicalities of art. With an open mind without expecting anything there is immense joy in admiring the art, I guess!"

"You are an interesting person, it seems."

"Oh is that so! Is this your first discovery in life?" Aruna burst into laughter.

"Will you care for a cup of coffee?" Asked William anxiously.

"Alright, let us cross the road," said Aruna as they came out of the metro station.

William was sitting in the cafeteria on the pavement right in front of Aruna, glittering like a diamond wrapped in red velvet. Watching at the stars in the sky Aruna remembered it was time for evening prayer. She joined her hands and offered them dedicatedly looking at the sky and then closed her eyes, the head being slightly bent down. Not that Aruna was religious but the beauty of the evening sky compelled her to do so. As she opened her eyes she found to her greatest surprise that William too was in a meditative pose – eyes were half-closed, his hands were folded near his chest as if an angel was emerging from the depth of mist to offer himself to whom he liked.

Aruna slept so peacefully that night in her studio. She had met someone who was there in her thoughts and the reality was so sharp and coincidental that she could not believe her eyes. She kept smiling standing in front of the mirror, gazed at the sky, looked through the window and kept expressing astonishment before she went to the bed.

Chapter 7

William returned to his studio. He had been staying in Paris for last five years. He belonged to southern France. Though his parents came to Paris quite often, he visited them at least twice a month. He was quite attached to them being the youngest among the three siblings. His elder brother worked in UK and his sister was married to a German, who lived in Frankfurt.

William took off his red shirt and placed it delicately in his closet. He kept watching his physique in the mirror. He looked at his biceps, at times thighs and finally turned around to examine his hips. He is very conscious of that part of his body. They must not look depressed. "The beauty of a man lies there so much! And not just in the chest muscles, as the pop thinking goes". William touched his butts gently and felt quite satisfied. Then he moved on to his studies. He had been working since past one year in a financial company. However, the habit of studying in the night at least for an hour or two before going to bed he had maintained regularly.

William lied down on his bed and he started thinking about Aruna. After all, she had a charm which was as spontaneous as her eloquence. She flowed like the river Siena - dynamic yet smooth. William imagined of giving a kiss to Aruna - an imagination of a typical European! He quickly got up and checked his diary. Yes, he had noted down Aruna's contact number. He must see her in the coming week and seek an appointment for a more extensive session to discuss substantive issues. Aruna must be knowing a lot about life, he fascinated. Innumerable questions were arising unconnectedly - how long she would be staying in Paris, had she been engaged with someone, would she like to take him to India someday and so on.

Suddenly the thought of his friend struck his mind. He had not met Dimitri for almost three weeks though the latter had been calling him almost twice a day. Dimitri worked in a bank and they had met two years back in a night club. In his thoughts he hugged him and pressed half a dozen kisses on his mouth. He was aroused. Held his instrument in his hands for a while and then fell asleep.

He met Dimitri the next evening. Dimtri kept on gazing at William while drinking coffee. At last Dimitri admitted, "I can't turn my eyes off you!" William returned it with a smile, "Come on!" They didn't talk much. William mentioned to him that he had met Aruna in an Indian function and he was quite impressed. Dimitri listened to him with keenness and wished him good luck. They took a walk along the lanes. Dimitri expressed interest to visit India. Before bidding good bye William pulled Dimtri closer and both went to an alley where he kissed him and fondled him. Dimitri tried to feel William without opening his flies. His finger kept hovering around the sensitive zones. He was getting excited to get into more serious stuff but William had to stop him as he was in a hurry to get back to his studio. Dimitri was not in a mood to let the opportunity go waste but William's plea could not allow him to proceed further.

William took the metro while Dimitri decided to hang around. Though he would have to go to work the next morning, he thought it was too early to be in. There could be more interesting happenings outside, he imagined. Given his vivacity it would not take him long to make friends. A sauna will be the place of last resort: if nothing worked he could expose and mingle.

Chapter 8

The next morning William called Aruna and sought an appointment for the following Saturday evening. Aruna readily agreed and both were looking forward to the meeting. William was wondering if both could spend sometime on the bank of Siena. But that would be too much to ask for. After all how little did he know Aruna! Still he kept on thinking about the possibility until it occurred to him that he could rather propose to Aruna to sit in front of Notre Dame and then gradually both could take a walk if intimacy developed.

Intimacy depends on both, not on one though one may take the lead. But then the other has to respond and reciprocate. Otherwise the initiative will be interpreted as imposition which in turn can destroy the future. William was intelligent enough to know all that. He was careful not to kill a petit tendril emerging from a young branch.

Aruna was not in the habit of using much make-up. Yet, before setting out for the meeting she stood in front of the mirror a couple of times. Perhaps she was too self-conscious that in front of glamorous William she might look dull. She had been reading off-late a book on Indian civilization, deviating significantly from the standard theories, and thought of carrying it to their meeting. Perhaps, William would like to know the details. Aruna herself had not published much on the issue but had gathered substantial materials. William must be having interest in the area, she convinced herself and wore a deep-necked top with a colourful scarf around her shoulders.

The conversation in front of the Notre Dame went on for long. Aruna kept explaining many other issues including the temple architecture and temple dance in India. Questions were enormous and answers matched them appropriately both in terms of content and depth. Darkness had veiled in long ago, both had not realized though. Suddenly William expressed his desire for a stroll along the river-bank. Aruna readily agreed and William took the opportunity to hold her hands. She did not object though she had not been in the habit of holding hands while walking. Something traveled from her palm to the brain and it was paralyzing. The space between her fingers accommodated William's, locked with hers, and the feeling was inexplicable.

Aruna felt a peculiar sensation as she walked with William hand in hand. She imagined a little more than what was happening in reality. William's desires were running wild too. But he had self-control. Aruna could smell the body-odor of William as he came close to her. It was intoxicating. For a moment she thought she would jump into the water. The whole evening was full of that odor, she thought. When she had returned to her studio she could feel the same fragrance in her body and in the cabinet door. She slept well but the same odor haunted her the whole night.

William called Aruna again the next morning in the pretext of knowing a little more about India. Aruna agreed enthusiastically as the spell of spring had started working on her. William too was so much drawn to Aruna that he enjoyed her company through and through and wanted to be with her again and again.

This time they went to Louvre together. On the way they stopped for coffee, and the discussion took a serious turn.

William was reviewing a book on poverty in developing countries. He wanted to read out certain portion to Aruna. She too was curious.

"The book paints various facets of poverty without taking recourse to the bright colours and exotic brushes of the aesthetic. Many have succumbed, yet many go on, for, the vigour of life is greater than death – doesn't matter even if life in the process comes to resemble the wrinkles of death more than being able to retain its own brightness. After all, life is an opportunity. And the poor will not let this opportunity go by.

Greed of one is deprivation for another. And thus the disparities in end-results are much more than what can be explained in terms of skill differences. Water flushed out of one household being utilized by another, the convergence of drinking water and sewerage and the co-existence of wealth accumulation and below subsistence level of consumption are indeed heart-wrenching. The book reflects on these tragic aspects of human existence."

Aruna intervened, took the book from William and quickly turned on the pages. Then she urged William to add a few lines she dictated.

"The day-to-day sorrows and joys of the households who remain in perpetual deprivation, who do not receive any attention of the rest of the society and whose struggle for survival is enormous, set the undercurrent of the book. Their ignoble strife, their potentiality to grow and shine, and their flexibility to adapt to the circumstantial changes are indeed noteworthy. These coping mechanisms are too unimportant for many who operate at the higher echelons but in terms of celebration of life they are not less important than any scientific breakthrough explaining turning points in human civilization."

William was completely spell-bound. He again returned to his own note after completing the lines Aruna gave.

"Without refusing life these individuals have accepted what they are not endowed with and have explored paths to keeping the body and soul together. The garbage pickers lying down close to the dustbin on the pavement and yet contributing to city's value added much more than what they are able to earn for themselves unfold greater truth of life than what the ever-remembered heroes could usher in. The tiny hutments even smaller than the doll's house of those born with a silver spoon in the mouth have been constructed with lifetime treasures – they are of no less importance than the historical monuments built by monarchs over the centuries. Ironically, though, the former can be razed to the ground within a fraction of a second without even bothering to know what they mean to their inhabitants. And this is pursued by those who are capable of having a greater sense of responsibility and conscience!"

"Excellent!" Said Aruna.

"Well, I should be thanking you for your time and contribution", William added quickly with a smile.

Then he continued, "You know Aruna, many of us are actually hypocrites and that is why there is so much of slavery and poverty in the world today".

Aruna added, "Freedom never comes without responsibility. Secondly, if one vouches for freedom for the self it should not be at the cost of others. Hypocrites are those who talk about their own rights but do not care for others who should also claim similar rights in similar situations. They know very well that their interest would be defeated if others would also enjoy the same avenues. But the good thing about it is that they cannot dominate for long. Very soon they are exposed as their concept of 'selfish freedom' is not able to deliver to the larger society."

William listened to her with expanded eyes. Aruna continued, "Hypocrites are those who try to provoke others from behind and fear to come to the forefront. If at all they come up they make sure that they have done enough homework to mobilize support through negotiations. But the principle of exchange or collusion of a bunch of people based on negotiations of selfish motives is not tenable. Notwithstanding their claims about honesty and high ethical values sooner or later people are able to disrobe their garb.

They always talk about strategies. When one fails they look for another. But can one fool a large majority for long merely in terms of new strategies? Life is much beyond strategies. In the process of inventing strategies they lose out much bigger gifts in life. The crooked mind cannot appreciate the beauty of the rising sun, for example. The amount of grace that a blooming lotus holds remains outside the purview of the hypocrites".

William added, "An immediate close attribute that this variety of people possesses, is jealousy. They try to prove their opponents wrong. And it does not matter even if they have to destabilize the system in attaining their goal. 'Self' is much bigger for them than the 'society'. Let the society suffer: as long as their individual image gets escalated they have nothing to care for. They try to step into the shoes of some personalities who the society has offered sincere respect but they fail to take note of the wider and self-less concepts which those individuals had preached and practiced".

Aruna returned to her point, "Freedom, selflessness, courage and responsibility are all inter-woven. You take out some of the set, the rest will not last. Activism with hypocrisy is a deadly combination. It can lure many but it is damaging and misleading. In reality activism often do not involve sacrifice as personal gains are of primary importance.

Democracy allows lot of space no doubt but there is always this fear that in the name of freedom self-interest can walk in and occupy the front seats. And that defines the death of democracy. Whether it is fight against corruption or revolt against extraction of natural resources the individual identity gets so dominant that it loses its significance and objective. Democracy allows every movement to enter but unfortunately the mechanisms the movement may take recourse to can be anti-democratic and democracy then lacks all instruments to keep it under control. Alone political institutions or economic institutions are not sufficient to deliver the optimum outcome. Somewhere there is the need for ethics. And this has to come from within. Even without any formal teaching there is conscience in us which responds automatically. How much importance we lay on it is a different issue altogether".

By then they were in front of a panting named "The Temptation of Christ" (1858) by Scheffer. The huge painting was on the wall and in it were Jesus and a naked male with wings, standing on a hill-top somewhere between Heaven and Earth. The naked figure with a muscular and seductive physique but with a terrible and crude face tempts Jesus to shift to the earth stretching his hands and fingers in the downward direction whereas Jesus, in contrast, completely covered in a gown except his radiating face, raises his hands and points his forefinger to the Heaven in the upward direction. Aruna could not move from the place for a while. Passion will always have a downward flow and divinity upward and one is situated somewhere in-between. This interplay of Passion and

Divinity is immortal and unending in human mind, she thought. She remembered the statue of Mahisasura-mardini: divinity kicking off passion with her left toe. Both Mahisasura wearing a brief and the naked man in the painting have repulsive faces though their body is attractive. This is the actual image of passion. "How articulately human mind has conceived passion!" Said Aruna to William. "But when passion is refined by love it can have an attractive face too", replied William. Aruna thought for a while and kept quiet. Both moved on to the other paintings.

Aruna after a couple of more meetings with William made up her mind that she was going to say yes if William ever proposed to her. William, on the other hand, was taking a lot of time to make up his mind. He shared a tender relationship with Dimitri and he did not think that he would be able to end it. Even if he would not pursue it with Dimitri what was the guarantee that he would not have such an inclination towards someone else in future? Of course that did not mean that his relationship with Aruna would be unstable. But the important question was whether such a double relationship of a man will be acceptable to Aruna. William had realized that it would be a futile exercise to hide the other side of his inclination, particularly to a lady who might be close to him or could be his would-be spouse. He knew for certain that it would not remain in the closet. So, he would have to take time to reveal it to Aruna and note her remarks, he thought.

Chapter 9

Somehow Aruna's appearance reminded Philip of his young days' girl friend. He started thinking about Aruna while sitting in the prayer hall. He tried to divert his attention but the thought returned with greater intensity. He came out of the hall and took a stroll in the courtyard. He went towards the farm and kept watching the animals. The birds were feeding the young ones. Philip felt a sensation in him: the affection that prompts to give oneself to others.

Again the image of Aruna appeared before his inner eyes. This time he felt, he was excited. Aruna's lips were like pink roses and they were close to his neck. He got a bit naughty and chewed her lips a little in his fantasy. The next moment the guilt feeling returned to him and he was apologetic about what he was thinking. He tried to utter the holy name several times. But his mind had already enjoyed the honey after consuming which anything else was less sweet or tasty. Life with celibacy receives the attack of passion with a much greater intensity than otherwise if celibacy happens to develop an ounce of weakness.

He went back to his residence and slept quietly. But he had a very disturbed sleep. Several times he got up. What is sensuous is strong as well, he thought. And what is ethereal is very mild. He covered himself with a blanket and tried to count his breathing, not to of much use, though. Then towards the morning hours he slept for a while but when he got up he realized he had nightfall. He rushed to the wash-room to clean himself. While taking off his trousers he got a hard-on and he recollected what he had witnessed in his dream when he had an orgasm. He imagined of having inter-course in different poses.

He had had no opportunity to meet Aruna in immediate future. However, after almost two weeks he saw her one day in the Indian temple. This time he came forward to greet her. Aruna extended her hands. Both took a stroll in the adjacent road and sat down beneath a tree for a while. Aruna noticed Philip's unusual muscular thighs as both sat next to each other on a stone. A tremendous urge to inter-mingle rose in her. She quickly diverted her mind. But Philip had noticed it in her eyes. There was something in him, pushing from inside, she noted. Various postures of copulation kept appearing in his mind. He was feeling as if his entire body was going to burst if he did not take Aruna into his arms.

Both got up simultaneously and started walking back to the temple. They talked about the Indian movies. Philip mentioned some of the comedies of recent make. Aruna had watched most of them and, therefore, could participate in the discussion.

As they came close to the temple gate the guilt feeling returned to Philip. He became very stiff, Aruna noticed. But she was behaving normally. She knew, she was attracted towards him but she tried her best to let the emotions flow low.

The Chief came out from his chamber. "Oh Aruna you are around!" He said. "Hope Philip took you around and showed you the vegetation we grow here".

"Yes, we have been moving around", replied Aruna.

He invited both in and offered sweets and fruits. As Aruna was getting ready to take leave the Chief suddenly remembered that Philip would be visiting Rome. He said quickly, "Aruna, why don't you accompany Philip to Rome? I am sure you will like to see parts of Europe when you are around. This will be a good opportunity for you. Instead of going all alone you can always go with Philip.

That will be more enjoyable, I am sure."

Aruna smiled gently and returned to her residence.

She reflected a lot on what the Chief had suggested. She decided that night to have the pleasure of having Philip's company to Rome. The next morning she called Philip and found out the travel plans so that both could do their advance booking together.

Almost after ten days they traveled to Rome. They went by train which took them almost eighteen hours as it was running behind schedule. The hotel was full they were told though they had had their reservations. The old lady at the counter claimed to have sent a regret letter which possibly did not reach Aruna and Philip. Anyway seeing them helpless she called her husband from inside and both tried for accommodation in the neighbourhood. They managed it eventually: it was basically someone's residence. But the inhabitants did not seem to be residing there and the place had been converted to a guest house. The old man booked only one room thinking them to be a couple. Philip was too embarrassed to say anything. Aruna made a quick request, "Sorry Sir, we need two rooms." The old couple looked at each other in surprise.

The rooms were very spacious. It appeared as if Aruna was in India. She opened the windows and placed her wrist watch and purse on the table. There was a beautiful alarm clock on the table. She had a bath and went to the park nearby with Philip. There they met several people from Bangladesh who were staying in the neighbourhood. One of the boys took the initiative and wanted to take them to Coliseum through a pedestrian route. They accepted his offer. The boy told Aruna that he had been married for last six months and his wife had not got a visa yet to accompany him. He was talking to her on his mobile every now and then while walking. It appeared as if both were in Bangladesh. He was teaching her some recipe, Aruna felt.

They reached the Coliseum after ten to fifteen minutes. Aruna was completely astonished to see the massive structure built almost two and a half thousand years ago. How developed the architecture was! They moved around the area for a while and then took a short cut to return to their hotel. The boy from Bangladesh showed them the ruins of some old buildings recovered from excavation and kept explaining that it was a very common sight in Rome. "Wherever you dig you will find the past of a civilization!" Aruna and Philip offered the boy to join them for ice-cream. But the boy declined. It was his privilege to take them around and he would not like to take any remuneration for that, he explained. Aruna tried to tell him that it was not remuneration – just a gesture of friendliness - but he refused. He was rather keen to return to his residence and have his evening meals – rice, pulses, fried vegetables and fish curry. He would lose his appetite, he said, if he consumed ice-cream before his meals. Aruna understood his modesty and felt very grateful to him.

The next day both went on a city tour in a 'hop in hop off'. They went to the Vatican and attended the prayers. After that both went inside the cathedral. Aruna was pleasantly surprised to see that in the sanctum sanctorum there is nothing but the light – what the Hindus call the *Brahman*. Aruna explained to Philip who relished it a lot. "The ultimate is the same in all the religions of the world", said Philip.

They spent considerable time at Spanish steps. Aruna saw a structure and it resembled the Lord Shiva of the Hindu myth. They took the staircase and went to the gardens around. It was very fulfilling Aruna thought. Both were engaged in serious discussions and kept educating each other. Philip was pleasantly surprised to note her knowledge on European history and could not help appreciating her. "After all I am a student of history; if I don't know this much it is a shame", said Aruna politely.

Chapter 10

The next morning when they were moving together Philip suddenly held Aruna's hands. She was slightly embarrassed but a quick current seemed to have passed through her body and mind she felt. She was not able to withdraw her hands. She enjoyed the touch of his fingers. She felt an extraordinary sensation as both the palms colluded. Their shoulders touched and Philip imagined as if he had a frontal collusion with Aruna, and her breasts pressed on his chest. He got a hard-on.

Aruna looked at the buildings all around. "They are called palace and they also look so", she murmured.

They visited the market; saw the stuff sold at the roadside, mostly imported from China and India and Bangladesh.

The following day they returned from Rome. They had a stop over at Florence. Aruna was enchanted to see Galileo's house. "The statue of David by Michael Angelo is one of the most wonderful things on earth", Aruna thought. Philip looked at the statue meticulously. Like Aruna too this is his first visit to Italy. Aruna noticed that Philip's eyes were fixed at the lower abdomen and the beautifully curved buttocks of the statue. She too had the desire of touching those parts of a man. She looked at Philip with lust and he noticed it from the corner of his eyes.

Before the evening drew in both were chatting in the railway compartment. They had a light supper. There was another couple from USA sitting opposite to them. The man looked quite old while the lady was pretty young. She was an NRI, Aruna discovered later. And the man was a professor of social anthropology in one of the universities in the west coast. Four of them talked a great deal about tourist spots in India. Aruna gave a detailed account of the historical places and went on emphasizing that it would be impossible to cover everything in one trip unless one would plan a visit of several months duration.

There was another old couple who lived in Paris. The lady spoke English. She took a lot of interest in explaining the details of French dishes to Aruna while she listened attentively.

Philip went to the upper bunk to lie down. He again had a restless night. Aruna's dark eyes, not-so-fair complexion and her long hair kept bothering him a lot. They were all falling on his chest and face the moment he tried to close his eyes. He tried again and again to take away his mind from all that was mundane he had thought. But he felt, what was mundane was an integral part of eternity as well. It was not all that easy to shoot off to a higher plane. "Perhaps it is the rule of the nature that one must pass through the basics before being able to reach the roof-top", he thought. He had to set his mind free. And he imagined a penetration with Aruna. The intensity of the feeling was so much that he ejaculated without touching his organ significantly. His brief was wet; he felt uncomfortable but he was too embarrassed to go to the toilet to change.

In the morning the train reached Paris. Both bade good bye the French way and left for the city metro in almost two opposite directions. Aruna kept thinking about Philip. The touch of his palm was still very fresh in her mind. Philip's personality had made a major impact on her.

Aruna had a bath and went to her study centre. She worked intensely till the late evening.

Philip was disturbed the whole day. He kept wondering about the vices and virtues. While people kept thinking about the possibility of his joining the philosophical centre he had been thinking about a woman and experiencing orgasm! It took him a long time to come to terms with the movement of his mind. At last he told himself, "If people think, I am a saint, let them. I must do what my inner self dictates". The Chief in the centre never asked him to renounce the world. He mentioned Aruna to his mother and she was enormously happy. She had seen Aruna in the Indian temple and had liked her very much.

As soon as Aruna came out of the reading hall she received a call from Philip. He almost said explicitly that he had very nice time with Aruna and she responded very bluntly by saying that she had fallen in love with him. Perhaps he was not prepared to hear it so explicitly or so quickly or he might have thought that it was a man's job to say so. He was quiet for a few seconds before he could return to the normal conversation on the phone.

"Oh what a nice to thing to hear that! I wish I had said it first. It feels so good to hear in this big world that someone loves you!" Philip exclaimed.

Aruna posed. Philip then proposed a dinner-meeting on the following Friday. Aruna accepted it and till then no one called each other. Philip of course confirmed the dinner invitation on Friday morning.

The evening was dazzling. The meeting point was quite close to her residence; she had decided to walk down. She was carrying some mementos collected from India. Philip was late by a few minutes. He had brought lovely roses for Aruna. He apologised for being late and then both settled down in a restaurant. Aruna noticed in him a unique combination of seriousness, mildness and firmness. All three made him radiating and lovable. He kept talking about his young days. And at some

77

point he did mention his girl friend in school. Aruna felt a little embarrassed: if Philip wanted to be honest with her it demanded reciprocity in return. And she could not decide if she would tell him about William at that moment. Philip's was past; so he could say it plainly. But William was there in Aruna's 'time present'. She kept wondering and could not decide what to say. However, before footing the bill Aruna insisted that they share. And she revealed in a very straight cut way that she had met William too in the India House on the day she had met Philip. Subsequently she had seen William a couple of times and without any hesitation she said that she was charmed by William.

Philip looked a bit dim though with his smile he tried to cover up his feelings. But Aruna's positive attitude and warmth did not allow his blooming love to collapse. Aruna took the initiative to shake hands with him and he quite spontaneously kissed her in the cheek.

Chapter 11

Slowly the days passed by. Aruna had to go back to India for a couple of months to do her field work. She mentioned it to William and he was a bit shattered. "I am going to miss you for next four months that means!" He exclaimed. He waned to know exactly when Aruna was planning her visit to India. Aruna said, "Sometime starting from the end of next summer. Now that I have got a fellowship for next three years I am delighted". William expressed a sigh of relief. Still he had three more months he thought for Aruna to begin her field work in India. "Anyway", he thought, "I will get more time to make up my mind about Aruna when she is away."

William met Dimitri more often when Aruna left for India. He wanted to have an assessment of the intensity of their relationship. He had to choose one between the two: his relationship with Dimitri or his relationship with Aruna? He liked both. He wanted to be with both. How could he settle with one and give up the other? These were some of the questions which kept bothering him. Finally, he concluded that he would have both if that would be acceptable to the other two parties as well. He was sure it would not be a problem for Dimitri. Dimitri possibly had many other friends and hence, he should be more understanding and must not be surprised about it. "He must be able to comprehend that it is possible to love more than one person at a time," William thought. "But how about Aruna? Will she be able to accept it though she seems to be quite broad-minded?" William would wait for Aruna to return from India and discuss on this issue with her. Aruna could sense a little about William's involvement with others. Aruna knew it was not possible for spring to settle down in one garden. Spring finds its victory as it moves on from one area to another. However, she was not aware of William's same-sex love.

Dimitri used to spend the evenings mostly outdoors. William for a while thought that he would withdraw himself from his friend and assess the reaction of both. But Dimitri was a person who would be the last one to impose himself on anyone. If William was staying away he thought it was because of his busy schedule. Even if he sensed avoidance he did not want to disturb him. He rather visited Peter and James with whom he had physical relationships too. He of course felt that he loved William more than anyone else. In his absence there was an emptiness in him which did not happen in relation to others, Dimitri noted. He did not miss them substantially though the physical part was as intense as with William.

One week-end he went to Burgundy with Peter and James and they had a wonderful time. But all through his journey he felt, he needed William too. Perhaps it would have been more enjoyable, more thrilling, more exciting had William been there! The feeling kept bothering him always. However, he had the decency not to call William and ask him bluntly as to why he was trying to avoid him. Dimitri in fact had seen the world more than William – he understood the value of intimacy because he respected privacy as well.

William had noticed this quality in Dimitri and was quite impressed. He thought it was quite unusual for a person who had an easy-go life and did not hesitate to entertain casual interactions. But Dimtri had depth and the ability to reach the bottom. He could understand others because he had understood himself very well. He would always say, "How little do we know of ourselves! When we do not understand ourselves well how can we dare to claim of knowing others though the greatest irony is that every moment we say, oh I know so and so very well."

Chapter 12

As soon as Aruna reached her home town Jaipur her aunt brought a dozen of marriage proposals though Aruna was deeply engaged in her fieldwork. Aruna's mother knew that she would flare up if she came to know the secret plans of her family members of getting her married. So she decided to keep quiet though the other members and Aruna's father insisted on discussing the proposals with her upright. Finally, Aruna's father decided not to bother her at least at that moment when she had been quite pre-occupied with her studies.

Aruna completed the transcriptions of the interviews and decided to return to Paris in next few weeks. That was the time when her mother could not suppress the temptation of discussing the marriage proposals with her. Aruna wanted more time and also indicated that she might find someone suitable in Paris. Her mother was shocked to imagine the latter.

Several new stories had come up in the neighbourhood, her mother explained. The most interesting component was related to Amit whom Aruna had known for a long time. How Amit was put to harassment because of his good-nature was the essence of the tale. Of course the central point was to tilt Aruna's mind towards Amit whom she had known since her school days. Aruna's mother started with a background to those who had been unkind to Amit.

Indu and Sumanta stayed in the same locality. They were married for more than a decade;

yet had no issue. Everyone in the neighbourhood gossiped about it. Some said it was because of the lust for career that the woman did not want to conceive. When there was time - she was young and had a higher probability of conceiving – she was too ambitious and that left no time with her to be in the family way.

With age Indu took to extra marital affairs after a vacuum started haunting her. Why was not Sumanta's company enough for her? No, Sumanta had left her behind long back, pursuing endlessly and uselessly to excel in the social circle without any dedication for diligence. A little bit of brightness everyone has but to be in the limelight for good reason one requires persistent efforts. Even brightness of super quality alone does not pay unless it is accompanied by endless strife for its explicit manifestation.

Indu flirted with her sub-ordinates. Her colleagues gossiped that she did not require co-workers but gigolos. The electrician while working on the lamppost peeped into her bedroom and saw her flirting with someone she had hired for office work. He conveyed it to Amit, a colleague of Indu and also a co-inhabitant in the same housing complex. Amit used to respect Indu a lot as his elder sister. It left no impression on him because the intensity of respect was higher than the depth of the gossip. There was lot of intimacy between the two not only professionally but also personally. In fact, when Indu joined the organization without much professional endowment some of the seniors had suggested her that she would need someone like Amit to help her establish.

Then came in Indu's life a guy called Mridul who was around fifteen years younger than her. Mridul an arrogant chap with some corporate experience thought of climbing up the ladder by taking advantage of Indu's loneliness. She too let her lust flow into the ocean of passion. Amit did not notice it until many others in the neighbourhood came to talk about it. But Amit ignored everything, saying it was her personal life.

Manu another employee of Indu, with absolutely inadequate IQ, however, felt quite jealous of Mridul. Without trying to realize his limitations he thought that Mridul was getting undue advantages. While he slogged hard day and night these smart fellows, he imagined, with some ability to communicate in English would move up with great rapidity. He came to Amit, who was helpful to him, keeping his economic weakness in view, and highlighted Indu's affair with the new guy. Amit gave a patient hearing to him but said nothing. "Amit must have analyzed implicitly the cause of his frustration", said Aruna's mother, "but with a smile he dismissed everything".

Manu's frustration did not go unnoticed by Indu. It reflected in his behaviour and work schedule and when Indu confronted him mildly but firmly he imagined a high probability of his dismissal and joblessness. Quickly he changed the topic and told Indu that Amit was saying certain undesirable things about her to him and he himself had no role in that gossip. Indu believed Manu keeping in view his loyalty he had shown in many occasions and turned cold towards Amit. The latter noticed it and ignored it generously developing an indifferent attitude towards all the individuals in the scene. But Manu wanted to play it very safe. He did not want to lose out on the benefits and support he used to derive from Amit. He visited Amit in one fine evening and admitted to him that out of sheer fear he had to communicate to Indu that Amit was the sole center of her character assassination. Manu also pleaded to Amit that he must not be annoyed with him for his lies because Indu could not harm Amit but could throw Manu out of the job if she knew the truth. Amit realized at once how foolish friends could be more dangerous than intelligent enemies. But again keeping in view

Manu's economic conditions he decided to remain completely quiet about the whole thing, allowing time to decide its course of action.

Indu in annoyance and frustration started ignoring Amit and one day while Amit was passing by she mocked at and ridiculed him involving Mridul as a collaborator. Amit noticed it and decided to distance away from them for good.

Illegitimate affairs grow rapidly and break all of a sudden too. But Indu was intelligent. As she realized that Mridul was eager to get married in order to push all the stories of their affair under the thick carpet of marriage, she too decided to end the physical association and pursue only the professional relationship with him.

"Marriage is the greatest institution that saves social criminals from being exposed, particularly in a conservative society", said Aruna. "It saves the culprits by giving them lot of space and by diverting the attention of the critics towards the singles," she continued. Aruna's mother could not say anything. After a pose she again picked up the thread of her story. It saved the face of Mridul and Indu too after their relationship turned into a professional one. Amit must have listened to his inner voice carefully and never let himself be a part of what people had been engaged with though given his intelligence he must have followed each and every incident and had a big laugh at all the developments.

Sumanta all these days had his own way of leading life. Tried his best to derive the maximum from every association of young women he came across. People used to notice the dismissal of maids every now and then from the couple's house but none suspected any illicit design. A new turn took place as Sumanta attacked their latest maid just before the wedding of Mridul. Thinking that she would succumb to his desires as he had rendered lots of material benefits to her family he insisted on a physical outburst.

Aruna stopped her mother. "But poor too have self-respect and they too deserve dignity. They too know that no magnitude of material wealth can match a forceful encounter. Rich understand very little of this, though."

"Yes", said her mother. "The maid protested against Sumanta's attempts and resigned from the job at their house."

Indu did come to know about these episodes of her husband's perversion since long but could not afford to challenge him as both were on the same track.

"Pretending ignorance and lending utmost support to each other in such situations work as the best shield in the name of broadmindedness", said Aruna's mother.

Indu calmed the maid by paying her generously and saved her husband's face, explaining to the society that he was too fastidiousness about every work at home and outside, which must have made the maid upset. However, she decided to discuss the matter with her husband later after the heated gossips died down. With critics being around, she might have thought that they would not spare her or her husband in any form if they could sense even an ounce of the whole incident. She wanted things to improve in the long run. At least they needed a very thick blanket to cover themselves. And the only solution, which could also bring both together with a common interest and keep the couple engaged, she thought, was to adopt a child.

Aruna commented, "Yes, what else can be thicker than the blanket of parenthood that can absorb dust of all kind and intensity?"

Sumanta, who had been quite tensed about the whole incident and looked for a desperate escape from the possible social disrepute and legal action against him, viewed his wife as an angel. The society would appreciate, after all, what a noble work the couple did pursue! Quickly he ordered for the latest fancy car in the market as a gift for his cooperative wife on the auspicious occasion of adoption. Indu also needed some respite and some new hope in the face of the vacuum that Mridul's marriage had thrust upon her. Soon the ceremony of child adoption took place with pomp and show

Amit learnt about it, and went to congratulate both for having contributed to this noble cause. But they decided not to open the door. On the contrary, they went around saying that Amit was causing harm to them and to their child. He was surprised but had the decency to withstand everything quietly.

Aruna asked herself calmly, "Is this adoption strategy a beginning of a new era for at least some of the ruthless couples, working out new ways of enjoying a secured future of having a permanent caretaker who would withstand all exploitation silently and relentlessly?" The answer could be in affirmative because the poor child did not carry the same gene of deception that was quite conspicuous in her/his foster parents.

Aruna's mother wanted to complete her story. Mridul's marriage quickly moved towards parenthood before his wife came to know about the past affair between him and Indu. However, after the birth of the child within a year his wife returned from her parent's home to join Mridul "The olfactory nerve in women is too strong. They can smell things even from a long distance". The body language between Indu and Mridul revealed more than what their efforts tried to conceal. Mridul's wife took a strong stand urging him to look for a change in the job. Indu protested. She said that in due course everything would be alright. "An illicit affair never dies", said Aruna's mother. "They used to go out in the pretext of work. The charm of her paramour to a woman is a thousand times stronger than of her husband". Thus it resumed and continued for a while till Mridul's wife had to stay firm to shift him out of the city. However, the worst part is that Indu kept on blaming Amit for Mridul's job change and left no stone unturned in inventing ways to take revenge on him.

At the end of the story Aruna'a mother went on, "It is better not to have friends than having such unscrupulous companions. Poor Amit had to face a great deal of humiliation for no fault of his".

Aruna knew each of the characters and that had motivated her mother to go on with great details. Of course her mother had an important objective in mind. She knew that both Aruna and Amit were great friends during their school and college days. That memory must have motivated her to narrate the story and expect in return a little compassion in Aruna'a mind for Amit. In case Aruna would feel inclined towards Amit and if they could be tied in wed-locks! Thus, went on desperate attempts to retain Aruna back in India!

Aruna understood everything. And that is why she could let her mother make some of those unpleasant generalizations. Her mother went on giving health excuses as well: she had not been too well; Aruna's father had pain in the chest and so on.

Aruna's father had sent a lot of money to Aruna, thinking that the fellowship money would be inadequate. Her mother had known this and was worried that the same could have been saved for her marriage. She was no exception; she thought as several other Indian mothers may think. Aruna's father of course had a vision and he could hold on to it because he always understood the value of education. He belonged to what we call middle-class – the class which had limited affordability for a number of important things in life about twenty years back but now has emerged with a significant progress in material transformations of their several interesting aspirations, though the relative position in the income-ladder might have remained the same.

Aruna did not pay much attention to what her mother was trying to indicate. Amit was a friend - perhaps more than a friend at some point in time. But that was okay. Then they had different paths – both had different objectives, both lived at a great distance from each other, physically and mentally both. What was the point in digging the past? She maintained silence. There was no point in arguing with her mother. From her point of view she was justified, Aruna thought. Every mother wants her children to get settled in life. The definition of settlement differs from generation to generation and from region to region. The inter-temporal differences are understandable. But the cross-sectional differences are incomprehensible. Whether it is geography or socio-economic factors one does not know for sure but certainly the differences are much more than what can be explained in terms of some of the mundane factors. Aruna looked forward to a human society which would be more homogeneous in terms of attitude. She believed in altruism and she knew that she inherited that quality from her mother. That is why she did not want to hurt her by revealing her little faith in marriage.

Her mother, she knew, was a gem of a person at heart notwithstanding the topics and the levels of her discussions she pursued. She represented perfectly the Indian middle-class. A number of defining characteristics of this class might have changed in last two decades or so but still certain other attributes remained the same. Money power, favorable attitude towards consumerism, capacity to buy education at a high price if the lack of merit could not help access it, the ability to pay for heath services and delay the death in case of exigency by encroaching upon the ICU of a private nursing home and the wide range of occupations which represented the Indian middle-class all have perceived upward mobility. Even then something concerning perception has remained the same at least among those who could witness the phases before and after the changes have occurred.

Chapter 13

The next day Aruna's mother narrated another episode from the neighbourhood possibly to reexamine her readings of her daughter's declining interest in marriage and other related issues. The reference point was again Amit.

One night Amit's colleague dropped a set of earrings at the common entrance of the group of flats where they lived. Amit's cook found them and he brought home so that Amit could hand over to the right person. The next day before Amit could trace the person who it belonged to the owner herself went ahead and shouted at the security guard, accusing him of having stolen the item. That was none other than Bilas's wife. Amit knew nothing of these developments. His cousin who was visiting him for a few days mentioned that while she was going to bed she saw a man with a child looking for something in the common passage. Amit immediately knew that one of his two neinghbours who had small children must have dropped it. He checked with one and she denied. Then he requested his cousin to check with his other neighbour, who was Bilas. Bilas's wife grabbed the stuff and wanted to know the details of how it was found. The young girl of ten – Amit's cousin - knew little Hindi/English and hence, she could only take the name of the cook who had found the stuff.

Amit thought that a great responsibility was over. But after a few days he discovered a strong letter written against the security guard, accusing him that he had stolen it and returned it to Amit out of fear after getting a heavy dose from Bilas and his wife. Hence, the implicit accusation was that Amit was unnecessarily hiding the crime of the security guard, who, as his neighbour believed, was a criminal. By helping conceal his crime Amit was actually encouraging theft in the housing society they lived in. Amit thought, all this said and done would have been fine had the security guard actually picked it up. But if the basic premise is wrong all inferences drawn thereafter are bound to be wrong. Sometimes a logical conclusion from a set of incorrect premises can be more harmful than an illogical statement deduced from cent percent correct premises. Unfortunately we always talk about logicality and not the importance of truth. Does this define the mindset of a typical

Indian middle-class even after being impacted upon by the positive economic changes that globalization has ushered in?

Amit considered the attitude sympathetically. He must have thought that his neighbour committed the fallacy of - 'after this therefore due to this'. He explained to the member of the housing society about the true happenings. The administration expressed tremendous annoyance with Bilas for bringing such false charges against the security guard. Amit was also a bit surprised to note that his neighbour put forth such a complaint without really trying to verify the truth. More shocked he became when he learnt that it was Indu who instigated Bilas's wife to do so. Disheartened he was to note that a person like Bilas who always talked about truth, justice and righteousness, was the one who allowed himself to be influenced by such miscreants. Amit kept discussing this incident with others because he was hurt, Aruna's mother rationalized.

The nature of crime committed by Bilas and Indu was very unique. For them poor did not have any dignity. They could be called a thief any time one had to explain a loss. If by chance it could be proved otherwise, they would then throw some gifts at them as a token of compensation. Amit was agitated and asked Bilas "What about their self-respect? The damage that is done by questioning their integrity cannot be repaired by whatsoever expensive gifts one may shower on them."

The miscreant of Bilas had a different purpose as Amit realised. It was his aspiration to supercede Amit for the coming election of the housing society, which he wanted to prove not in terms of efficiency but by showing Amit low and dishonest. But in the process he did not bother to smash a helpless guy. Whose crime was bigger, Amit kept wondering about it and of and on discussed with Aruna'a mother. Also he realized that people had already warned him against Bilas, yet he had continued his friendship with him thinking that he had a genuine feeling for the poor. He might have had true feelings but jealousy and dual nature superceded the grain of goodness he contained.

Bilas's wife is a careless woman with careless attitude towards others. As the summer months approached there was load-shedding and shortage of water. So there was the need to pump the water to the overhead tank. But whenever she switched on the pump she forgot to put it off at least before six/seven hours and that too only after someone in the neighbourhood pointed out. Amit being the immediate neighbour did so consistently and patiently though he realized after a while that she might be finding it like a reminder from a nagging mother-in-law. After some time he completely ignored and left the task to her realization. But the situation did not change and it must not change until the doer was willing to learn from the mistakes. Days passed by and the wastage of water, electricity and noise pollution continued.

One evening Bilas's wife switched on the motor for the whole night and put up the same careless attitude. The whole night Amit suffered as he could not sleep because of the noise the pump created being located just near his bed-room. Next morning as he got up he could see a pool of water in his garden overflowing from the overhead tank. He decided to bring this to the notice of the authorities.

As the authorities communicated to Bilas not to waste water and create inconvenience to the neighbours, he flared up and in return wrote a strong letter accusing Amit of being unfriendly and uncooperative. Also his allegation came against Amit's television set and music system being too loud, and to prove his point he asked the authorities to cross-check with other residents in the same locality.

Amit was taken by a surprise. How come

other neighbours supported Bilas when they had been appreciating his music all the while and requesting for positive externalities. But then Amit must have understood the collaboration between Indu and Bilas. Indu's true nature must have flashed before his inner eyes, and he went up to her directly. When he asked her to tell him if she had got disturbed by his music she looked baffled for a while and then answered, "Depending upon my mood I might have said something of this kind". "But you are the one who came to me and borrowed my cds after you enjoyed the externalities. You are the one who requested me to raise the volume so that others could enjoy as well!" Amit said. She kept quiet but quickly gathered courage to say that it was better to listen all by oneself rather than playing it for others. Amit returned home with a blank face, "Why do these characters play such dirty games?"

"Amit is too simple to realize that the best way to get someone into problem is to ask him to do something that his enemies hate", Aruna's mother added. Indu had mastered this art very meticulously.

Chapter 14

Aruna did not pay much attention to what her mother kept saying. She knew Amit was a good person but there was no point in getting into the daily trifles. The neighbourhood problems of the Indian middle-class are in themselves the very definition of the middle-class. In spite of the rise in real incomes there is an endemic problem right at the bottom. Un-adjusting nature, visualising a non-issue as an issue and extensive discussions on petty matters and the efforts made to prove oneself of being highly principled comprise the pass time engagements. Aruna reflected on this a bit and smirked on realizing that she herself was a part of it. She wanted to visit Baby in the neighbourhood though she had never met her before.

Baby had moved to their locality just a few months before Aruna came to India. Despite her hoarse voice and galloping walk like a horse she tried to look feminine and also smart by wearing western clothes. She pursued her career somewhere in Madhya Pradesh for sometime, and then on realizing the low prospects of acquiring lucrative jobs she quickly changed over to a subject that provides shelter generously to anyone who seeks entry prematurely or over-maturely, promising equal prospects to all to be able to reach the top if one is at least gifted with the power of eloquence rather than understanding.

For having such dreadful ideas about a discipline Aruna looked firmly at her mother and aunt who had joined in the mean time to dissuade her from visiting Baby.

But according to the family members of Aruna Baby lacked this talent of playing with words and so she had to take recourse to other means. She could not pierce her nose in three different places, nor could she provide the same treatment to her ears and decorate them with ethnic rings and stones to come to the limelight. She looked for a fellowship to travel to a country, which certainly offers a rubber stamp of elitism to every native who drops in even during transit.

But scholarship was not adequate to provide her a decent living. On the other hand family background was a little above the lower middle class though most of her family members gave a look of even less than the class they represented. Baby's looks of course resembled a typical Indian utensil, which, in spite of being half-burnt, did glitter due to the magic of the washing powder.

Baby decided to look for Indian guys abroad who went from a decent background and supposedly would not have much expectation from her. Sameer was working in the corporate sector. Hailing from a very learned background he was smart yet modest and had enough income to spare after feeding himself adequately. This was what Baby was aspiring for all these days. Soon she decided to move into Sameer's flat. At least she would save a lot on the housing front!

The living together concept worked quite well. Baby concentrated on her research and soon completed it while Sameer spent most of his leisure looking after the household. Grocery, cooking and cleaning were his main occupations after his hard work in the office and bringing himself to terms to translating Baby's transcriptions.

After her studies Baby thought of returning to India and insisted Sameer to seek a transfer. By then they were married. Though Sameer enjoyed the monopoly of what he was doing abroad and envisaged adequate promotion prospects he quickly decided to make a compromise with everything, given his modest nature. Thus, life in the national capital began.

Baby was more into liaison than work. She threw parties to get tenure. Sameer cooperated as much as he could. Once the requirements to reasonable extent were met on the household front he thought of asking his parents to come and stay with them. Being the only child of his parents this much he thought was his duty towards his ailing and aging parents. Baby was all these days imagining the ecstasy of having multi-partners. Her passion and her sexuality both were seeking an intellectual freedom. She was thinking of getting rid of her husband, and as an irony of fate that was the time when suddenly arrived the responsibility of in-laws on her! She counted stars in the broad daylight. "I must give an ultimatum to my husband", she thought. But how would she do it or say so to a man who had never said 'no' to her? Disagreeing with those who disagree is easier than with those who are always agreeable. She decided to take long leave and go away to Indore for field trip. She chose this city where her husband could not accompany, as there was no branch office there. Her husband, as usual visualized this step of Baby as a strong move towards her career achievement, and supported it earnestly, thinking that his parents could afford to postpone the care they expected to receive from their daughter-in-law for a while. In the mean time he thought of serving his parents himself by asking them to come and stay with him.

Sameer did all the packing, took the clearance of all the bills and papers that Baby had left behind. A few weeks passed after Baby attained the satisfaction of having settled all the dues in Delhi. Then slowly she came out – she decided to do what she wanted to do. From a distance showing ingratitude to those who oblige is easier than being in their company.

Baby's divorce papers reached Sameer. He kept gazing at the sky. Where did he go wrong? What did he do to receive this kind of a treatment? There was no problem from his side in terms of expectation since he could easily revise them and keep them in favour of the partner's interest. He had recognized no feeling of in-satiety in Baby either. Of course the freedom she was seeking was beyond the domain of his conceptualization.

He requested, coaxed and cajoled for a withdrawal of the papers but nothing worked. His tears did not have any meaning for Baby. All she had to say was that it was not working anymore and hence, it was desirable for both to stay apart. Sameer was too naïve to think of all he had done for her and to get angry. He pressed a little by saying that divorce was never followed in their family culture and it was going to bring a lot of disgrace. After all, what was the need for them to go for a separation when he was willing to accept any charter of demand she could put forth! Baby did not want to reveal the efficacy of the concept of her freedom. She simply dismissed him.

Things went on in their due course. Sameer quietly succumbed to the pressures Baby exerted and decided to withstand all social humiliation and personal agony though he did not provoke anyone. Baby's joy knew no bound. She would do whatever she wanted to pursue. It was alright to think so but where was the need for her to disturb someone by entering into a marital relationship with him? This was what many thought in the neighbourhood when Baby came to stay in Jaipur after her divorce. Her plight to Indore was only a plea to excuse herself from Sameer. Later she thought it was too small a place for her life's celebration.

Aruna had to listen to her mother for a while on these issues after she mentioned her desire to meet Baby. But her mother's efforts to stop her from having any social-interactions with Baby were going to fail miserably.

Neighbours felt that Baby's multi-partner-ecstasy started in full-swing. As youth was not going to last for ever, everything had to follow at a rapid pace. Sex-liaison promised her major promotions - at the end she hit the real path to success. She emerged as social elite, throwing parties every now and then, making her rooms look the way she imagined paradise. She ordered exotic dishes for the guests she invited with special care and comfort. Aruna got a bit fed up with such comments from her aunt.

She even paid no heed to what other neighbours had to say about Baby. She made a courtesy call which Baby returned in no time. Both developed a close friendship. Aruna found lot of interesting things in her. Baby was extremely helpful to Aruna. She accompanied her to several government offices to get the approvals required for the fieldwork. "What motivated her to call off the marriage is no one's business", Aruna told her mother. "She must have had enough reasons to justify her stand. After all, the freedom of the sky cannot be understood by the rotten ones in a cage!" She told herself.

Chapter 15

The next day Baby took Aruna to a lecture at India International Centre in Delhi. It was on a Bengali writer Ashapurna Devi. After the lecture both had coffee and talked a great deal about the writer's less known work. Baby had good knowledge in Bengali literature. She was carrying the special issue of a magazine dedicated to the writer and read out several passages to Aruna. The article was in English so Aruna didn't have much difficulty to follow. Baby of course went on explaining and translating certain Bengali terms wherever Aruna had difficulty.

"Poverty and women are two closely connected themes in developing countries. Even in households above the poverty line, not to talk about the poor households, intra-household inequality of resources and consumption exists considerably, leaving women at the lower end. Besides, women-headed households are more prone to poverty as they lack resources to pursue productive activity and as biases of the society against women are at times irreconcilable and fall outside the realms of all tolerable limits. Ashapurna Devi being one of the most humane writers of the contemporary age, has focused on this theme in various ways with her sharp intellect, in-depth feelings and skillful articulation. While laying considerable emphasis on women issues in general, the 'poor woman' with low social status and inadequate resource base takes a special position in some of her work." Aruna explained.

She again started, "Ashapurna Devi's *Izzat* is a glaring example of the vulnerability to which a woman of poor economic status is exposed". On Aruna'a request she narrated the story briefly. "Basanti who has been appointed by Sumitra and Mohitosh since last four months wants her young daughter to stay with Sumitra as Basanti and her daughter both are terrified by the social evils in the slum where they reside. Her other employers have not obliged her, and finding a small family as that of Sumitra, Basanti is quite hopeful. Sumitra understands Basanti's problem and tries to extend a helping hand. However, Mohitosh, as he learns of such a possibility rejects the proposition mercilessly, imagining unnecessarily that Basanti and her daughter may be up to bigger games of blackmailing the couple, i.e., taking the fullest advantage of Sumitra'a generosity Basanti and her daughter may put up false allegations against Mohitosh indicating that he has held up the daughter, and thus extort money".

"The author has shown in the story how low economic status translates itself into poor social status as well," intervened Aruna, recollecting the allegations she had heard against the security guard in their neighbourhood.

Baby posed and then continued. "Basanti's daughter is exposed to humiliation in her own locality and at the same time she is subjected to gross insensitivity of those who are higher up in the socio-economic ladder. Sumitra and Mohitosh are in a position to help her out but Mohitosh's careless and casual attitude leaves

Basanti and her daughter in pure indignity and shame. Mohitosh doubts the genuineness of the problem that Basanti and her daughter face; however this suspicion does not arise from a genuine sense of fear of getting black-mailed by them or their neighbours. The fact that he spells out his doubts without contemplating upon the issue is testimony to this. With poverty, in his eyes, are associated a bunch of ethical evils which he has imagined effortlessly without trying to give any benefit of doubt. Mohitosh is only a representative of the upper class – what Mohitosh perceives is indeed what the upper class visualizes".

"Even if one accepts for a moment that whatever Mohitosh told Sumitra was absolutely possible in this uncertain world, particularly keeping in view the growing crime rates in a big city, it is still difficult to side with Mohitosh", said Aruna.

Baby added enthusiastically "And this is mainly because of the way he expresses himself." She then read out to Aruna a few more lines from the article: "Forget those poetic sentiments! Retorted Mohitosh, heatedly. You must act after the proper consideration. I've seen the girl. A girl like that can't remain good in such low-class surroundings."

Both Aruna and Baby looked at each other. "How poverty particularly in a woman-headed household can take its most vulnerable form, how the lack of resources can be so conveniently equated with lack of a moral character and how social rejection and segregation exist even in an inter-dependent social system are brought out emphatically by Ashapurna Devi."

After listening carefully to Baby Aruna added excitedly, "At this point let us turn to Kathrine Mansfield's *A Cup of Tea*. "Rosemary, a young woman of large fortune was absolutely devoid of feelings but her greed for fame and name had driven her crazy to bring the beggar maid (Miss Smith) home. She wanted to adopt the poor girl not because she was genuinely struck by her poverty but because Rosemary thought that that would pave her way to publicity and popularity. Her husband, Philip was absolutely aware of this attitude of hers and also knew the practical problems of two different social classes, suddenly inter-mingling and merging to become one overnight. However, he showed immense maturity in dealing with the situation. He saw to it that her wife's not-so-genuine sentiments did not take a tangible shape and at the same time he made sure that no one was hurt in the entire process. His tactfulness must not be interpreted here as his cunningness rather it was his in-depth understanding of the situation without sounding inconsiderate and rude".

Baby smirked and said, "Ironically in *Izzat* when Sumitra says, 'This means I have to tell this maidservant that I have no say in this household', Mohitosh reiterates in an inhumane way, 'And what a person before whom your prestige is going to be shattered!'. Since poverty is seen to have no self-respect in the eyes of the society, since a poor has no identity, and rather a poor woman is believed to have poor moral standards as well, how does it matter if Sumitra loses her prestige in the eyes of such poor creatures! Reduction of a poor woman to something of gross insignificance is indeed a hard reality which the author has brought out so spontaneously and straightforwardly".

Aruna and Baby went to Utopia to have snacks. After coming out both sat on the staircase and again started the discussion.

Baby said, "Basanti's daughter has questioned in her own insignificant way the social dualism and rejection. 'That's enough Ma. Come away. There's no need to cry and call on Boudi. It's clear who has the last word in this house. You are not to fall at their feet, thinking of your daughter's *izzat*. The babu's don't care about the *izzat* of a low-class girl. All right. If we are low-down people, we'll have to settle for a low-down life. If we have to go to the dogs then that's what we'll do'. The egoistic attitude of Mohitosh has, however, failed again to hear the agony of the inner spirit of a helpless poverty-struck girl. He interprets it as a reflection of pure uncivilized attitude. Be that so, does the male dominated society (Mohitosh) has all the monopoly right to behave arrogantly? The author has brought out skillfully the hypocrisy in Mohitosh's character. If he believes in speaking himself the naked truth bluntly he must be prepared to hear with an equal magnitude of sportiveness the other side of the truth from someone else. But unfortunately that is not the rule of the world".

"But the unfavourable attitude towards poor women is not merely shown by males in the society", Aruna said anxiously.

"Yes", replied Baby, "even persons of their same sex are at times unduly unjust. From this point of view Ashapurna Devi has no gender bias: In the story *Tamonasher Bhramnash* (Breaking the Illusion of Tamonash) she has created Bidisha the main target of whose verbosity is "*akarmar dhari*" (useless girl) addressed generously to the house-maid, Sonali Mondal, an inhabitant of a village in 24 paraganas. Bidisha's all allegations and attacks under the sun are generously directed towards this little girl though Tamonash finds her the perfect house-keeper in all possible ways".

Aruna was enjoying the discussion. She thought for a while and said, "I don't think that woman to woman contact means a lot in terms of support to each other."

"You are absolutely right", replied Baby. "In fact, the other point which comes out very sharply in her work is the domination of one woman over the other which in an external sense may appear to be close alliances between women. These relationships are not necessarily of great affection. In spite of Tamonash's sympathy for Sonali she tries to maintain a distance from him. On the other hand, she expresses her loyalty to Bidisha notwithstanding the ill-treatment mitigated to her very often. The author has not accepted this closeness as pure love between women rather she perceives a great deal of fear leading to subjugation of one woman to another; thus loyalty that is being shown so conspicuously is a function of this subjugation: *'Ki eta? Swajati prem? Na swajati bhiti?'* Being a lady I think it requires a great deal of courage to realize this and more importantly acknowledge it so explicitly, as Ashapurna Devi does, thus creating a special position for herself as a purely balanced person in the feminist world".

On their return Aruna'a aunt asked her a lot about Baby. She wanted to know if Baby was leading their innocent child to the path of devastation. When Aruna mentioned her depth of knowledge to the family members, the women folk were stupefied like owls. Being judgmental can be self-damaging.

Chapter 16

Aruna returned from India managing successfully not to entertain any marriage negotiation. By then many in the Indian temple had started suspecting her relationship with Philip. That was because Philip himself went around appreciating Aruna every now and then.

Nina was a middle-aged woman who looked more like a man than a woman. The listener went either mad or deaf if she caught hold of someone to express her views on issues she thought were of great concern. Problems might have been of great importance but they were highlighted by her as per her convenience or to suit her interest. The whole administration was a failure, all her colleagues at the work place were corrupt except she herself and her close friends, if at all she had one, were some of her major complaints. All the while she was engaged in critcising someone or the other. A perfect epitome of causeless malignancy! Hence, it was difficult to know if such persons could actually identify a genuine issue or it was all cooked up stories. Very few therefore dared to come close to her when she visited the Indian temple in Paris.

Every time she laughed the listener could easily imagine that a man was hiding behind a lady's garment. Her voice and her delivery style resembled that of a trade union leader. The interesting part was that after talking non-sense for hours without any coherence or consistency and break she thought she was genuinely gifted with tremendous oratory skills. On the contrary, all she had was an untiring energy to speak illogically for hours together. A loud mouth with very little content!

To Nina no one was hero; everyone had tremendous weakness, just by touching the feet of the seniors they had climbed up the ladder. When she talked all this sheet to others they listened patiently with a feeling of pity, "Poor lady does not know what she is speaking, God forgive those who do not know what they are doing".

Negativism can actually lead to madness, every time one curses someone else causelessly, invites nothing but inevitable curse for oneself. Every time she screamed, it revealed nothing but the echoes of deep frustration, foolishness and insanity with prominence. She was a clear-cut pathological case. Notwithstanding all this Saurav tolerated Nina and respected her a great deal. Many had warned him that she possessed two heads of a black cobra but he had laughed it away when he had decided to marry her some twenty years back.

Nina looked at Aruna in the Indian temple when both incidentally were visiting the centre one day. She wanted to start a conversation but Aruna did not give her much scope. They were in the lecture hall and that was not the place for socialization, Aruna indicated. So Nina had to hold on to her curiosities until they came out and reached the dining space. Nina wanted to know if Aruna was married. Exactly at that point Dharitri an elderly lady emerged from the crowd and with a twinkle in her eyes asked Aruna, "So how is it going with Philip? The other day I came to the temple and learnt about it", she explained. Nina got the material in bulk, more than she had expected. "So this Indian woman is in love with a French guy!" And then followed a series of lectures on disadvantages of international marriages. Aruna was getting bored. However, her modesty did not allow her to speak anything rude. She kept nodding her head without uttering a word.

As an opportunity came her way she quickly disappeared in the crowd. But this time she was caught by Suarav, Nina's husband. The man was obnoxious, Aruna thought. He was trying to flirt with every young woman he met. Aruna did not smile back when he came and introduced himself. He was trying to invite Aruna over dinner. Why she should accept the offer, she thought. Of course the pretext was that he would like to discuss some of the research issues that Aruna was pursuing. Since he himself was an architect it was not all that easy for Aruna to dismiss him right away with an excuse that he would understand nothing about her research. She managed to keep him at a distance for the time being.

The next time when she visited the Indian temple she learnt that the man was dead. And there was a gossip all around that he had committed suicide. She saw Meena after a long time whom she had met in the metro station during her first visit to the India House. Meena took her to a corner and explained how the man was tortured by his wife. Not even a cup of tea his wife ever prepared in her life. Both were engaged in remunerative jobs but the household had to be managed entirely by the man. Even when the poor fellow slept the lady would scream at the top of her voice if she wanted a glass of water. Some time back when he had a fracture in his right arm, the entire household survived on junk food for two months but did not initiate cooking. "On top of all this the amount of misbehaviour she offered generously to him, my God! Every now and then she used to abuse him. It is he, who has taken such a long time to take this decision. Had there been someone else he would have killed himself long ago or would have left home", she concluded.

"Yes, too much of tolerance can be due to lack of self-respect!" Aruna commented spontaneously.

Aruna felt depressed. Perhaps the man was only trying to be friendly with her the other day which she misunderstood for being flirtatious. Her reciprocity could have helped an innocent survive. "A little friendship, a little warmth, a little kindness we always lack", Aruna thought. She felt very guilty about the whole thing and returned to her residence without waiting for the snacks to be served.

Chapter 17

Philip visited the Indian temple and the adjacent spiritual centre regularly. His work load was quite heavy. Every evening he was there at the time of worship. Aruna always found him quite a cheerful person and she too started visiting the temple every other day on her return from India.

It was a special day — a large number of visitors were around. After the prayers Aruna sat opposite to Philip in the dining table during lunch. He noticed that a young lady, who would perhaps be younger than Aruna, was sitting just next to Philip. She looked terribly upset with marks of tears in the corners. It did not take Aruna much time to realize that something was wrong and it must have been in relation to Philip.

Philip, on the other hand, talked occasionally to this young lady as he was talking to others as well. He took no notice of her tears, remained busy in serving others while eating from his own plate occasionally. "Good", Aruna told herself, "duty for duty-sake. Philip does not forget to attend her and find out if she needs anything, but at the same time he has been so indifferent to her that she didn't even notice her tears".

A little later Aruna saw the young lady sobbing continuously. There was so much beauty Aruna noticed in this dropping of tears. Tears of spiritual love! Philip was like Goutama the illustrious one — indifferent, determined and calm!

This young lady Alice had been visiting the centre since last ten years. She had met Philip in this centre several times. Philip was quite friendly with her too. But as he grew up and became closer to the head of the Centre his interest in spiritualism became so intense that at some point a possibility also emerged that he might join the order. Philip did have a strong desire to join the centre for good but he was asked to observe his feelings more closely and critically before taking any final decision. He had been put to test whether his life for spiritualism was sustainable or it was only a matter of passing phase. Ever since he had started thinking about this possibility he had cut down on all his friendly talk with Alice. He did not avoid her but at the same time he maintained a great distance from Alice which she was able to feel through and through. And later when he was getting driven towards material life it was Aruna who was at the centre. All the more reason for him to stay away from Alice. What an irony of fate!

Aruna took a bit of time to understand that she had sensed it right: Alice's misery was connected to Philip. On asking the Chief about who Alice was the Chief told Aruna that Alice had been interested in Philip but because Philip was contemplating upon the possibility of joining the order both maintained distance. Aruna felt miserable, "What if the Chief comes to know that in the mean time both she and Philip had come close!"

Aruna's respect for Philip increased as she thought that he did not take advantage of Alice. But at the same time a peculiar sense of distance started growing in her mind taking her away from Philip. Though her heart had started growing closer to Philip she increasingly felt that Philip was quite unattainable and even if he would decide one day to combine spiritualism with worldly life then Alice should get a greater preference over anyone else. Alice who loved him quietly waited for him without demanding anything and only wept when love hurt her. Her suffering must have a bigger reward than anyone else, Aruna thought. However, conscience and hearth both do not converge always. At the same time Aruna discovered that she was thinking about Philip, was imagining as if they were married and was fantasizing as if she was in his embrace. Aruna said to herself, 'This is called illusion or *maya*. Even after knowing that Philip was beyond achievement her heart still longed for him and kept hoping against hope consoling that anything could be possible under the sun. Life is an uncertain road, which turn it will take at which point at what moment is even not known to God for sure. God may not be a dice player but he is not certain about the outcome either. Prayers and determination can change the destiny. But then why Aruna was thinking on those lines? Did she want Philip, and if so would that be at the expense of Alice? "Poor Alice, innocent Alice!" She snubbed her mind for being selfish.

Aruna had struggled with herself several times in the past. It is the tendency of the mind to be weak first, but then rationality is the biggest attribute that human beings have been gifted with. The fire of rationality would burn all the illusion into ashes.

Chapter 18

Aruna did not talk much with Philip that day. Perhaps he was a bit upset to see the tears in the eyes of Alice. She returned to her apartment, a long way from the spiritual centre. She kept thinking about the west and the east. How the east is changing so fast! When she was young, things used to be so different. And now the younger generation – she meant even those who are younger to her – is so different. She is caught somewhere in between, somewhere at the cross-roads. She had seen the last phase of the old system and she is now reaping the fruits of the new system. But are all the fruits of the new system really sweet! She did not want to think about all this too much. She was having a splitting headache. "Does not matter even if all the fruits are not sweet. One has to live in one's age and thus has to face all the outcomes – sweet and sour both. Everything cannot be tasty and desirable. If we want something better we should be prepared to have something worse as well because it always involves risk. And nothing in this world is risk-free. Moreover, in absolute sense nothing is fully bad or good. A combination will emerge, it depends on the proportion. If a larger proportion is good, then nothing like it."

Aruna lied down for a while. Alice's face was appearing before her inner eyes over and over again. She turned her face towards the window and tried to close her eyes. The children in the next door school were screaming at the peak of their voice. Aruna otherwise would have found it highly disturbing. But then she enjoyed it somehow. "In the free and uninterrupted expression there is so much joy!" She thought. She rested her hands on the pillow and kept combing her hair with her fingers. Suddenly she heard a murmur below her window. She raised herself half and from the bed itself tried to observe outside the window. Hers was a first floor room on the roadside though it was only a narrow lane - hardly any vehicle crossing throughout the day. Two grown-up males – must be in mid-twenties — were engaged in a lip-lock while their hands were eagerly touching each other's private parts. Aruna got a little jerk. She had never seen it before, though had heard a great deal of it. Of course it was not a public display of passion. The males must have found the ally a bit secluded and did not imagine that someone might be watching them from the window.

Aruna called up William the next day and spent the whole evening with him. William as usual appeared quite attractive, perhaps a little more than earlier. He too took a lot of interest in Aruna. This time he looked more confident and more determined to continue his relationship with Aruna. But had he ended his association with Dimitri? No, not at all. After maintaining distance from Dimitri for a while both met the other day and spent the whole day together - in the night they made a great deal of love before going to bed. Well that was not his first time with Dimtri, but after that whenever Dimitri appeared before his inner eyes, he felt a sense of pleasure — a sensation in his whole body which he liked most, he was often aroused. At the same time he wanted to be with Aruna. Whenever she called, he found lot of excitement in him. In fact, he came with so much of interest and keenness to meet Aruna that day. Aruna's hair locks were falling on the left side of her forehead and looked like the patches of dark clouds around the moon. He felt like playing with those locks. He asked if he could hold Aruna's hands. Aruna shied a bit but did not object. "Let things happen the way they should happen. There is no point in obstructing", Aruna thought. She was not a baby that she could not understand William's interest in her. And she too had been attracted towards him quite a lot. As they got up to come back again to the restaurant after buying a few things Aruna saw several pairs of eyes revolving around William. Several of them took note of his beautiful and proportionate hips. A perfect physique to be framed and kept near the main entrance of the living room! He is no less than one of the statues in Louvre. In fact, he exactly looked like the statue of Mercury except the fact that the statue has a missing penis. But enormous rays of grace emerging from the entire body! The face is so calm and charming! The boyish yet intellectual sharp look is simply maddening! Aruna kept appreciating without expressing a word.

She was getting driven to William so much so that she did not realize whether it was she or William who had pulled the chair to sit in close proximity of each other. The dim light inside the restaurant was absolutely matching the sequence. William tenderly drew Aruna's face closer to his and kissed her lips persistently. Aruna did not withdraw. For a moment she forgot everything. She felt herself in the hands of cupid. She forgot those eyes which were admiring William when they had stood up to go out. The world did not exist for her. Only she and he! What a moment of eternity it was!

Slowly she returned to her senses as the waiter poured some water into their glasses. She could not miss the passion with which the waiter stared at William. By then Aruna had become quite experienced in terms of witnessing such same sex eye-contacts and more. So she was not surprised. She only thought if William was equally curious to respond to the desire of the waiter! Was he trying to hide it because she was present? She took the pretext of going to the loo and kept observing William, standing behind the curtain near the cash counter. Yes, she was right. William reciprocated with an equally passionate look. Aruna was a bit tensed and perturbed too. She returned to the table and quickly normalcy prevailed. No, she must ask William directly about his sexual orientation. If he said he was bisexual what would Aruna say, she was perplexed for a moment. As no prompt solution appeared in her mind, she decided to postpone her query. Again she engaged herself in thorough intellectual discussions with William and in the process kept feeling that she wanted him desperately.

No, her existence could not be complete without him. She herself offered to give a kiss to William this time.

Chapter 19

The next day Aruna got up quite late. Her observations of the previous evening on William and the associated suspicions which indeed were making her indecisive about him had put her off. Towards the evening she came out of her studio and slowly strolled over the wooden bridge over Siena. At the horizon the golden setting sun was sluggishly disappearing. Parts of the river had turned into liquid gold. Aruna could not set her eyes off the scenic beauty. There near the barricade Aruna saw her landlord standing with his huge camera of sixties/seventies model. He did not want to miss this opportunity of seeing the golden ball and preserving it for future use. Who knows maybe just a few more such evenings would come in his life! Like the evening sky slowly engulfing the earth, little by little he too was approaching darkness. Who would know when everything would be absolutely dark! At least till he reached the end he would be able to witness the golden ball — the symbol of life — if he could capture it in his small gadget. He worshiped life and he would do so till life had not ceased to exist in him. When life had more time for him, he did not have much time to spare for this. And then when life was about to exit he could find time to churn out the essence. One thing Aruna understood was that she must celebrate every moment in life. Even while standing at the last stepping stone in life this old man had not forgotten to utilise the opportunity of drinking nectar with both his palms spread out. Let life spread its wings as much as it can! For, it cannot come back again. An opportunity for once and all.

Aruna called William the next morning. His face was too bright in her heart to be forgotten. She remembered his possible associations with other males but could not ignore his charm. Passion is too deep to be ignored. Aruna called Philip as well. The peace in his face soothed her grief that lied in the depth of her unconscious self. In the turmoil, peace of course gets the victory which comes quietly without any humdrum. Passion on the one side and peace on the other kept filling Aruna's mind to the brim. Aruna was not getting torne in between. She found complementary relationship between the two. One image was accompanied by suspicion, possessiveness and insecurity while the other offered calmness, patience and steadiness. Aruna was too involved to realize the individual effect. What she experienced was a balance — a balance that exists in the centre and that is why life goes on; does not break down even when the chariot of the body is crushed. Aruna had read somewhere the theory of multiple existence.

Aruna went to the City University. From the park in front of the university as she strolled down slowly she entered into a lane — Rue de Nansouty (property private). The display of enormous beauty in the most generous manner kept her mind captive for long. The plants all around the walls of the houses looked so lively that Aruna felt peace personified. She imagined as if she entered one of the houses in the lane. She could hear the music overflowing the buildings and the lane — she felt as if she herself was playing upon a violin. She could see the kitchen and the dining space in the first floor from the road.

She imagined, she was sitting on the window watching the hanging garden in the house opposite. She was talking to several of her relatives many of whom were not alive. Thoughts were overflowing her mind. The Ganges, the city of Benaras and the evening *arti* at the banks of the Ganges which she had the opportunity of watching only once in her life, crossed her mind. She was too engrossed to understand the reason and ask herself why in Paris suddenly the Ganges had appeared. Why such convergence of such divergent objects? What unknown beauty had awakened her inner-self which connected all those appearing apparently isolated! 　　　.

Aruna found much strength in her to face the reality — to respond to both the poles of attraction simultaneously. By not letting her mind being bound by restrictions she had learnt all through her childhood she could find much joy. Let time decide the course of action instead of letting herself being torn into pieces by too much worries and thoughts that could not lead to any action. At times the state of mind in action without much thought can be better than the state of mind in inaction but flooded with too much thought.

Sitting under the shade of a huge tree in the garden in front of the City University campus she looked in the upward direction. The tree, branches and leaves all joined to form an envelope around her existence, she felt.

The leaves appeared as if they were made of marble. Then in certain parts a couple of outlets she could see, through which the deep blue sky was distinctly visible. It looked so unique. Distance hides all unevenness. All odds and unevenness can look plane. The asymmetries look distinct as one comes close. And these asymmetries then result in enormous differences again leading to distances. And these distances provide space to repent on committed mistakes in the process of which the asymmetries disappear and glimpses of evenness starts appearing little and by little like the morning sun. Thus is the secret of the sustenance of the human relationship cycle.

Aruna looked at the tree again. What a wonder nature can do! All bulges, all erections, all unevenness pushed themselves into Aruna's mind to eliminate the vacuums of depression. The dense forest, trees standing close to one another in incompatible rows and columns leaving no space in-between made themselves appear in Aruna's mind in a manner which was free from all void, emptiness and all pathos of a vacuum.

Life is never entirely useless. Even when it is useless and appears like a closed chamber outlets are there. Through these outlets something other than what is mundane, something more than the daily trifles are visible. Life is not boring. Life does not cease to explain its persistence, she thought.

Aruna met William again in one of the restaurants near Chateles. William's warmth was intense making everything appear in

Aruna's eyes absolutely charming. She forgot the contradictions she had thought to have observed in William. Both enjoyed their drinks and subsequently ordered for some food.

Aruna looked around: the neighbourhood was male-dominated. She realized that the neighbourhood was full of people who possibly had inclinations towards same sex. She felt a bit uncomfortable. She thought she would ask a couple of questions to William in this regard. But hesitation stopped her. She went on talking about India to William and with all keenness William listened to her. The journey to eternity along the stream of Ganges and her many tributaries in the depth of the unending chain of mountains of the Himalayas started conversing with William as Aruna's narration gained momentum.

Both were deeply engrossed and had almost forgotten their presence. The delay in the arrival of the food due to the heavy demand of the customers on a Friday evening had provided space to both the conversationalists. William was holding Aruna's hands in a strange awe as she was describing the Alaknanda and Mandakini, and the sound that the rigour of the water flow produced.

Suddenly appeared Dimitri from a small lane opposite the narrow road, with a bunch of young men all smoking profusely. Dimitri's attention fell at once on William sitting with Aruna on a table at the pavement – the logical extension of the restaurant. And there was such a great exuberance of joy and greeting each other that Aruna was completely frightened. She collected herself quickly and reverted back to the present from her Himalayan expedition. By the time she looked up towards Dimitri he was already hanging or the back of William who in the meantime had stood up to welcome his friend. William's face was glowing in joy. So was Dimitri's. They kissed each other the French way. But Aruna felt, their lips too touched while placing cheeks against one another. Other young men also greeted William and they were all watching him intensely. William was extraordinarily charming, they thought. William forgot to introduce Aruna to the rest. However, Dimitri realized who she was and after saying hello to her decided to leave William in peace to entertain his special guest. But while departing he fixed an appointment with William for the coming Wednesday and this time Aruna saw quite explicitly that William and Dimitri kissed on the mouth, a short one though.

Aruna did not want to suppress her curiosity, worries and tension any more. "What is it?" She must find out from William. Whether he wanted Aruna or someone else? More fundamental for Aruna to know was whether William wanted a woman or a man forgetting entirely that William may be seeking both.

She asked him directly, "William, are you interested in him? I thought we were ....".

William shied a bit and than said very openly, "Yes Aruna I have been trying to tell you very frankly. I know Dimitri for last several years. We have had sex as well. We like each other.

He is much more to me than a friend. However, ever since I have met you I have felt an inexplicable attraction towards you as well. I want to be with you and if destiny does not forbid I would like to spend the rest of my life with you. I have tried to assess myself over last several weeks: whether all this is just infatuation or something much more than that. I have felt an unavoidable inclination in me towards you, which touches the cutting edges of both emotional and physical planes. But also let me tell you honestly, I have not been able to forget Dimitri and he continues to attract me more or less in a similar manner".

William was continuing but Aruna stopped him abruptly and exclaimed, "But how's that possible? How can you have both?

William said, "Well theoretically it is

possible. But in actuality, I will have to try if I can forget Dimitri and have my inner urge only towards you. You must give me a chance. Aruna was disturbed again to hear William. But his last two sentences brought in some pleasantness in her mind. She was pleased with William's frankness and honest confessions and also to learn about his possible efforts in her interest. Without saying any word she nodded her head, perhaps more as a sign of being agreeable than expressing her understanding. Both settled the bill and bade good bye without wasting any word.

Chapter 20

The next day Aruna met Dimitri by chance in the metro near Gare du Nord. Dimitri recognized her at once thought he had seen her only briefly. For Aruna it was difficult to have forgotten him. First she thought, she would look through him. But then that would be very indecent, she corrected herself. They were almost face to face in the coach. Dimitri smiled and greeted Aruna, extending his hands. Aruna reciprocated well. Dimitri took the initiative to ask her destination and on learning that both were heading towards the same stoppage he requested if she could join him for coffee. Aruna agreed hesitantly.

Dimtri started the conversation, "I look

forward to going to India someday soon. I am very fond of Hindi movies too".

"Do you follow some of the small-screen soap-operas?" Asked Aruna.

"You mean to say Indian? No, I don't think those channels are very distinct here except one or two serials which are telecasted by other channels for the foreign viewers. But a friend of mine from India had recorded and brought here a large number of episodes of two or three serials and I had watched them at her place".

"And what are they?" Aruna enquired.

Instead of answering him directly Dimitri said, "Many criticised Ekta Kapoor's women-centric serials and ultimately the channels had to take a strong stand on not broadcasting them. In fact, several of the critics were women themselves. But now in retrospect it appears that people actually failed to understand what she was trying to depict."

"For example?" Aruna asked snobbishly.

Dimitri continued, "In spite of affluence and achievements and being able to move to the top, women are not able to come out of the typical mindset that prompted them to nag each other. The conflicts within the household continue even when there is no dearth of resources and as women tend to become careerists the outside world too witnesses considerable spill-over so much so that the proverb is, one successful woman cannot stand another. This message was certainly not taken in a positive spirit as it portrayed a very poor picture of women in the society."

Aruna found his deliberation quite interesting. She added, "The rifts within the households among women who stay absolutely confined to the narrow domestic walls can easily be attributed to the patriarchy. And thus, there is not much to explain".

Dimitri intervened, "However, when it comes to those who are highly qualified and have a professional career it is certainly a pity. Of course some of the feminists still may like to relate it to the politics of men, women simply being its prey. But one can cast several instances in which women have exhibited pettiness even when men are not present in the scene remotely. And these are some of the instances which require a solid explanation. Several studies have shown that women have not been less corrupt than men. On the contrary, given the scope, women have actually been more proficient than men in certain negative activities."

"Possibly they are less risk lovers and hence, not too many such instances actually can be observed", Aruna said sarcastically.

Without paying any attention to what Aruna said Dimitri continued, "Similarly when it comes to cruelty, records exist to indicate, some of the women have undertaken acts of greater intensity than what men generally can pursue. Two hypotheses emerge very distinctly: one, women are more serious in what they do – positive or negative. And two, the mindset of women does not change rapidly. The second hypothesis is worth pursuing.

From the psychological point of view actually it takes several generations to nullify certain practices and habits because it has taken several centuries to make them as a part of existence. This is true of all human beings. Something has been imposed upon women for ages and they have developed certain responses accordingly. All of a sudden if we expect a so-called successful woman to behave in a completely different manner, it would be highly erroneous. What has been forcefully coded in the genes cannot be erased overnight. So Ekta Kapoor was justified in bringing out meanness among the successful ones as well."

Aruna became serious, "Everyone is liable to make mistakes."

"But certain judgmental errors are gender-specific irrespective of social, economic or intellectual background. Such mistakes are natural to happen as they have not been exposed to complex circumstances repeatedly. The sensitivity of the rest of the society is important, therefore, in understanding the true causes of such pitfalls rather than blaming women."

Aruna was getting drawn to the depth of discussion.

Dimitri returned, "But the issue is serious when a woman holds an important and responsible position and may be liable to commit certain mistakes unknowingly. Naturally in such circumstances the fate of a number of persons is at stake. What should be rightfully done to reduce the damage? The most important step in this regard would be to stop her from pursuing what she wants to. Whether she will be able to realize her mistake or not is not the question. Most probably she will not. But to save others this step has to be initiated at any cost. There have to be mechanisms to counteract the vindictive pursuits. When women talk about empowerment of women they hardly realize that in reality only a handful actually benefit and more importantly, because of their empowerment a hundred get completely disempowered. Moreover, the irony is that the empowered woman becomes so self-centric that she actually forgets the main issue that she has been working for. Such cases are overwhelmingly large in every sphere, ranging from politics to bureaucracy and academia. In fact, how many vulnerable women have actually benefited from any women specific law compared to the plethora of cases of misuse of laws by the empowered ones!"

Dimitri stopped, thinking that Aruna might have been hurt.

She understood it, "No Dimitri, please continue. I am liking your ideas."

Dimitri smiled and said, "Oh I didn't expect so much, though. Anyway coming back to my point, who should be engaged and consulted in making policies for women is definitely an important challenge. It has to come from the grass-root level. Their inputs to policy making will be more pragmatic and effective compared to what their empowered counterparts may think on the basis of their intellect. The duty of those who take the initiative will be simply to collect the information rather than trying to add any viewpoint. Let not activism supercede. Description at times is more meaningful than profound research".

Aruna was thoroughly impressed. They had another round of coffee and Dimitri insisted on footing the bill as the invitation had come from his side. Aruna returned to the library and reflected more on Dmitri than on the issues they discussed. "After all Dimitri has a mind, has an independent view which is neither male centric nor a repetition of what he might have heard from feminists".

She again told herself, "Yes, William has a reason to be intimate with Dimitri".

She went for a walk and felt a bit angry with

herself for having been unkind to Dimitri in the beginning, "So what, if William and Dimitri have any special relationship?" She had come to know William only since past few months. It was too much to expect that William had been waiting for her since past life. "What William might have thought when I spoke to him so meanly the other day?"

Chapter 21

Aruna met Philip in the Hindu temple the following weekend. Philip was eager to talk to Aruna. The solemnity of Philip's face kept Aruna absolutely attentive. Both talked so much about India that at some point they forgot that they were in Paris. Philip wanted to know the details of the Himalayan expeditions. Aruna went on endlessly. "Both Philip and William have so much commonality in terms of interest and yet they are so different — one is like the southern breeze of spring and another like the deep clouds of the rainy July; yet they converge", Aruna thought, particularly in the plane of her own mind.

Aruna noticed that Alice was standing at a distance. She quickly greeted her and in response Alice came running to Aruna. Philip felt a little awkward, Aruna assessed, and he tried to move on to another group of Indians. But Aruna didn't let him go away. "No, Philip you be with us. We both want you to stay."

Alice blushed, Aruna noticed. "She cannot stay without Philip — the painful feeling is absolutely evident in her face. Yet she is not able to say so?" No, Aruna must do something.

After a while when they both moved on to the dining hall for dinner, Aruna without any hesitation and without beating about the bush asked Alice straight away, seeing no trace of Philip in the vicinity, "Do you love Philip? Yes, you do. I can see it. But then why do you avoid him, you don't talk to him?"

Alice put her eyes down because they were growing watery. "Yes you are right. I don't avoid him he avoids it seems."

"But why?" Aruna enquired. That's because he wants to become a monk.

"Non-sense, I think she has lot of interest in women and in a householder's life."

"He might be having but he wants to overcome all that and join the centre as a monk."

"Come on, I will convince him."

Aruna next day called up Philip and wanted to have a serious discussion regarding Alice. Philip did not pretend anything. He admitted that he had been aware of Alice's feelings towards him. At the same time he mentioned that he wanted to pursue on the lines of spiritualism. And at the end, he said that he liked Aruna, which was more than a mere liking though he was hesitant to use the term love.

Aruna was a bit confused, "A person who is so serious by nature is talking about so many possibilities! Is he lost? No, given his steadiness he cannot be confused".

"So you have three items in your mind right now," said Aruna a bit jokingly. "Spiritualism, Aice and me?"

"Yes, that's right. But I know I cannot pursue all three" Aruna could not say anything. She wanted to state that spiritualism and one of the other two can go together. But then which one between the other two? If she said "Alice", she would have to forget Philip for which she was not ready at that moment. If she said "Aruna" then it would look too selfish she thought. Silence was the best response in such complex situations. But silence is no solution. She must think about it later.

The whole night she was awake. Alice's face was constantly appearing before her. "Such a quiet girl with a pair of sincere and loving eyes! There is so much beauty and yet so much pain in her face". She must convince Philip to marry Alice. And for Aruna Philip could stay as a good friend. Of course, it was not all that easy as said. Aruna's feelings for Philip was no less serious. Particularly after hearing from Philip that he too had a strong inclination for Aruna, it was indeed difficult for her to make the sacrifice so easily. She was feeling more driven towards Philip. She had not realized when the night had slowly slipped out in the whole process and dawn was about to set in. The morning breeze from the window of her living room entered her bedroom and she knew not when she fell asleep.

Chapter 22

Next time when Aruna met Philip it was almost after a month. Philip came up to Aruna right away and expressed his desire to spend his life with her. Aruna was a bit surprised because she had not expected it and that too in such a straight forward manner, rather in an unromantic way. Philip said that he had thought about it a great deal and had made up his mind. He would pursue spiritualism and Aruna could be his co-passenger in that path.

Aruna felt extremely glad but she was reminded of Alice. Those painful eyes appeared at once. How could she ignore her and go ahead with Philip. "Philip you must think of Alice", she said, "I am delighted to hear what you said to me. But you cannot ignore the sincerity Alice holds for you. Even I am not sure whether my feelings for you are so intense or not. Can you place your hands on your heart and say that you don't have any feeling for Alice. Such a wonderful girl! It is simply impossible to ignore her."

The impression of an innocent girl shedding tears quietly and sweeping the floor of the worship hall flashed before Aruna. People had left the remains and the thorny stems of the bouquets on the floor after decorating the altar without bothering to note that the stuff could hurt someone and, moreover, might spoil the beauty completely. On the other hand Alice was clearing them with all sincerity. Philip was so much deep down her heart that his aloofness had caused her enormous pain. It is indeed a torture when one falls in love with someone to whom it cannot be expressed because of the person's indifference!

Philip said, "We will talk about it later".

'No, Philip you cannot afford to talk about it later. It is very important. I don't mind if you don't talk to me for the rest of your life. But I cannot simply withstand that innocent girl's suffering. Philip realized Aruna was serious. It was not generosity. It was justice that Aruna was trying to seek for Alice.

Philip was at one point quite friendly with Alice but ever since he noticed that she had been in love with him, he started avoiding her. Well earlier the ghost of spiritualism had possessed him entirely. Later when he found compatibility and complementary relationship between spiritualism and romanticism, he chose Aruna. But Aruna would not allow it to happen. "Do you mean to say that I should then pursue with both of you?" Asked Philip quite jokingly.

Aruna didn't know what to say. On the other hand, William had asked for time to make up his mind. So William was not available cent percent to compensate for Philip's loss. Yet, Aruna did not think about her self-interest.

Life is not always to grab! There is a lot of pleasure in accepting something as it comes and leave it where it ends. There is no need to carry it all along. Aruna had the self-confidence and the mental strength to be without anyone. She loved someone but that did not mean she would possess the loved one like her undergarments. She quietly took leave of Philip.

Philip too kept wondering as to what he should be doing next. Should he get back to Alice? But he could not forget Aruna either! What complexities of human mind! "No, Aruna is right. Alice is a wonderful girl and it will be completely wrong to say that I did not love her", Philip kept worrying. He thought to sort out things in the next few days.

Chapter 23

Aruna decided to meet Alice the next day. It was a sunny day. Aruna and Alice were having coffee sitting in one of those pavement-cafeterias at Saint Michael. Aruna without delaying the main issue came to the point directly.

"Alice, you are in love with Philip, aren't you?

Alice looked at Aruna quietly. Her eyes became watery with the mention of Philip.

"No, Alice I don't want to embarrass you. But I want to tell you a couple of things very frankly. I too admire Philip a lot. There is a unique dignity in him which has a spell-effect.

He and I have dined a couple of times. In fact, in one of the meetings he suggested to spend his life with me. Of course I was flattered. Who would not like to have such a wonderful proposal? But Alice, believe me, the first thought that struck me as he mentioned, was you. I have seen love in its purest form in your eyes. Of course I love him too. But I cannot grab something you have desired quietly. I cannot make myself happy I know for sure in such a situation. And it is in my interest I tell you this rather than being generous or something of that kind."

Alice broke her silence, "He is very lovable. But whenever any possibility came up of being close to him, I felt that he wanted to pursue in the path of spiritualism and he appeared quite averse to the idea of leaving a conjugal life of a householder".

"No, Alice, I think his thoughts have undergone lots of changes. He has made up his mind to give a tangible shape to his feelings. Otherwise he knows he can't be happy with his spiritualism alone when desires keep pressing his heart all the while. More importantly, he does not think anymore that spiritualism and love are mutually conflicting. I have seen him and I have seen you too. Both are associated with the same spiritual organization. Both of you have a great deal of commonalities. I think he has realized what you think is right: he has learnt the mutual compatibility between love and spiritualism from you. You and he converge over a very large space".

Alice smiled quietly and hesitatingly said, "I

am too scared to initiate any discussion with him in relation to my feelings.

"No, Alice I have already talked to him, He may get back to you soon. If he does not then I will talk to him again".

"You will, I am sure. But tell me Aruna you too love Philip as you yourself admitted now. Why will you forgo your share for my sake?"

Aruna smiled, "Yes Alice you are right. It is difficult to ignore Philip, particularly the way he has captured my heart: But still I feel my feelings are nothing in comparison to yours. You must have what your heart longs for and that is what my heart keeps speaking with its every beating."

They did not talk much on the issue. Both took a long stroll along the coast of Seine, almost till the evening. They kept watching the musicians and the dancers displaying their talent at various hotspots of the long stretch. They laughed and at times sang together, had two/three rounds of coffee, also sat down in the garden adjacent to the Notre Dame Church. Both admired the architecture. Alice explained some of the themes in detail to Aruna, while Aruna kept admiring the statue of Mary, an epitome of sacrifice. Aruna's whole self entered a peculiar state: she felt as if the earth beneath her feet was sliding and she was gradually gaining height from the ground. Aruna enjoyed the feelings to the brim. "These are uncommon incidents," she told herself.

Chapter 24

Alice mastered courage to call Philip. He was not prepared for it though. It was quite unexpected, particularly given Alice's nature. In the last so many years of subtle interaction Alice had hardly called him. Philip was anxious in case any unpleasant think had happened. Alice very softly told Philip that she had had a chance to meet Aruna. Philip understood the context. He quickly said, "Yes I too had a chance to talk to Aruna. She has lot of intuition and understanding of the situations and persons".

Knowing Alice for such a long time Philip knew that it would be difficult for him to discuss anything over the phone. For, Alice speaks more through her expressions than words. He expressed his desire to see her soon and with that he ended the conversation.

Next when they met it was on a festival day in the Indian temple. Alice was cleaning the fruits and arranging them on the plate. She had already prepared the other plates with sweets. The flowers were placed in the vase perhaps in the most decorative manner.

Philip had come from the back door. So Alice had not noticed. Her attention was on the front door as the Chief had asked her to welcome the guests. Philip greeted her with a big smile and Alice, while still cutting the fruits sitting on the floor, looked up and with a pleasant surprise returned his smile. Philip started, "Alice you are a wonderful person. I think we both know each other's feelings for a long time. It was my fault that I could not make up my mind. And now when I am prepared to share my life with someone, both you and Aruna appeal to me a lot.

Alice was perhaps not prepared to hear such a remark. Whether the statement carried any optimism or it was a kind of consolation used by the judges in the reality show for a failure was not known clearly. Her lips expanded slightly though not really transforming into a smile. And then she again put her head down, trying to complete the unfinished task. Philip went on, "No, Alice I have quite a lot to discuss with you. I must have you as my life partner."

Alice was not expecting this. In joy and shyness she almost collapsed. Philip went up to her and took her hands in him. By then

Alice was already in tears. So much of joy like thousands of suns shining on glaciers of pain which then had started melting into multiple streams flowing down with great rapidity! Her quietness said a lot. Philip assured him to talk more on this issue later.

Alice returned home with a great delight and narrated the whole incident to her mother. But somewhere in the bottom of her heart there was an awkwardness making her uncomfortable like a thorn pricking her fingers while holding a bunch of roses. Philip did say that both Aruna and Alice appealed to him. But he had chosen Alice! That's because he could not have both. Aruna had also mentioned to Alice that Philip had almost proposed to her. And Aruna's persuasion probably compelled Philip to return to Alice.

All that was fine. But it was getting difficult for her to accept the fact that Aruna would be out. "But then one of the two has to be", she thought. This is the way of life.

Aruna could stay as a friend to both Alice and Philip. But somehow the concept of sacrifice kept bothering her. Philip liked both and he would have one of the two! Aruna would quietly step back, Alice knew. And Alice would accept the sacrifice like a typical heroine of a novel. Well if she did not like this outcome she could then leave Aruna and Philip together and distance herself away for the rest of her life. If she would not want Aruna to make the sacrifice, then she herself would. All these thoughts kept bothering her so much so that she became absolutely confused. A sense of guilt prevailed in her.

She started convincing herself that she was doing something wrong. She decided to think about the matter again before taking the next step. She sent a SMS to Aruna saying that she would like to see her the following day.

Before Aruna could actually get an opportunity to meet Alice, she had to leave Paris for a study tour. She went to a couple of countries and then thought of visiting her parents in Jaipur. Her parents again talked about her marriage. She avoided the entire discussion, saying that she did not come home for marriage, rather just to see her parents. If they wanted to see her again in India then nobody should talk to her about marriage. Sadly her parents kept quiet. The daughter was grown up. She was engaged in higher studies. If she did not want to talk about her marriage she obviously could not be forced into it. Her parents wanted to explore if she had anyone in mind. But she said nothing and thus the matter could not receive much green pasture to grow. Well, they thought, how many of their relatives after all had been leading a happy life after marriage. If she could remained composed in her own way it was fine.

Aruna went to south. She admired the temple architecture and prepared an article on *chola* dynasty. She decided to present it in a conference in Nice. The body of the paper was not too satisfactory she felt after completing the first draft. She wrote it a couple of times sitting in the temple premises on the Chamundi hills, in the outskirts of Mysore, till she was satisfied thoroughly. Perfection was something that Aruna had learnt to rely on. Before anyone else the self should be able to enjoy every bit of what one does. For Aruna life was also like writing an article. She herself must enjoy every part of it before expecting others to like it. Therefore, she preferred to apply her judgment in deciding what was good and bad rather than accepting what others forced on or offered to her. She received Philip's proposal but thought it was more enjoyable to see Philip with Alice than herself. If she wanted she would have entered into a marital relationship with Philip, leaving no space for Alice. Philip was not the kind of person who would pursue an extra marital affair. She got William but seeing his passion for Dimitri she gave freedom to William to make up his mind. If she wanted she could have bargained with William. She could have said, "If you want me, you then have to forget Dimitri". And William must have agreed to her condition though it was difficult to say whether he would have kept his promise or not. At least to marry Aruna he might have theoretically accepted the clause, Aruna knew. But she had her own ways of determining happiness. Thus, she bestowed ample freedom on William.

Chapter 25

Philip and Alice met again in the library of the spiritual centre attached to the Indian temple. Alice was curious to know about their future. Instead of talking much Philip invited her to visit Auvers-sur-Oise with him. She readily agreed. It is a small place with enormous beauty all around. Van Gog had lived here during the last days of his life. A wonderful tree in bloom stood in the premises of the house where the painter had passed his last breath. Alice and Philip kept admiring the gardens of the residents there. Philip had already made arrangements to spend a couple of days at Auvers. One of his distant relatives had a house there. But they lived in London, only occasionally came to France. Philip had talked to them and had received the keys by courier. Both saw the church and the wheat fields which acquired a significant place in the work-space of Van Gog. Towards the evening they moved to the house after wandering the whole day.

The house was a bit dusty, but well-maintained. Alice organized the room. Philip lied down on the carpet as he was too tired. Alice was still in the kitchen preparing their dinner. After some green tea Philip felt fresh and he joined Alice in the kitchen.

Alice started, "It is very kind of you Philip to think about me."

"Yes, Alice I like you very much. But I have been quite confused about the whole thing. I was not able to decide".

"Decide what?" Alice thought Philip would mention the trade-offs between his spiritual pursuits and his human feelings.

But Philip did not go that way. He straight away said, "Well between you and Aruna."

Alice didn't like the answer.

Look Alice I must admit that I have liking for both of you and of course I could choose anyone between the two. And in that case I might have preferred Aruna. But she insisted that I must not make you sorry. At the same time I don't want to lose her either. Now tell me frankly if you can adjust to this idea that we three go ahead?"

Alice was not prepared to answer this question. She had never imagined of such a possibility. Yet, she said, "Yes". The fear of losing everything must have prompted her to say so. Moreover, she was grateful to Aruna. She knew what Aruna had done to put them together much before Philip told her this. Maybe she thought one day Aruna would go back to India and then Philip and she would have a proper married life. "But what happens if Aruna does not return to India?" she did not want to think much on those lines. She was madly in love with Philip. If she did not agree she perhaps would have had to stay without Philip for the rest of her life, she imagined. Now that she got some hope why would she lose it, fearing the uncertain future. She recalled some of the deliberations at the spiritual centre of the Indian temple. Let her not spoil the present, she admonished herself.

Alice slept in the bedroom and Philip in the

living room. Both got up in the morning and went for a walk. Alice was walking a little behind Philip. Suddenly she became emotional and hugged Philip from behind "Oh Philip I will die without you". Philip gently moved her to the front and kissed her lips. "I am so grateful to you for your love," said Alice.

Philip knew the difference in the love of Aruna and that of Alice. Both were not the same. Alice with all her existence loved Philip and she would do anything to make him happy. Still there was something missing which Aruna alone could fulfill. And what was that? Philip was pondering over it. "Yes", he got the answer. The wave length of Aruna and Philip matched perfectly. Human beings cannot be satisfied with sincerity in love alone, he thought. There has to be communications beyond love. And if such a relationship can develop between two to indicate convergence beyond love then nothing like it. No, he could not forget Aruna, he said to himself.

He did not elaborate on this to Alice. But in plain and simple words he tried to communicate that he would continue with both. He had understood that Alice would not be able to refuse it. And at the same time he thought it was Aruna who motivated him to accept Alice's love and therefore she must not refuse him. But the next moment he thought perhaps Aruna wanted to sacrifice her love, wanting Alice to be happy. "No, that is not acceptable". He must speak to Aruna about this when he would get back to Paris. He became impatient. He had grown suspicious that Aruna probably ended her relationship with him for the sake of Alice.

He could not wait until they returned to Paris. Aruna was not in France, he remembered suddenly. He called her up after Alice fell asleep in the night and came to the point directly.

"I have accepted Alice as per your suggestion, Aruna. And we are now visiting the outskirts. But please assure me that your relationship with me does not end."

"No, of course not," said Aruna.

But Philip thought it was an expression of modesty or it may mean only friendship.

He wanted to be sure on that. So quite bluntly

he said, "I am talking about our love relationship Aruna. I want to give a tangible shape to it. To me you are in-substitutable".

Aruna did not know what to say. But she knew she also loved Philip and there was something more than love between the two. She did not hesitate to agree with Philip. Reassured and delighted Philip fell asleep. However, he kept thinking that one day he would convince Aruna to marry him. By then Alice probably would resign and retire from the business of three-some. She was not the type who would be able to accept this in the long run though in the short run she might have agreed helplessly. Philip was also not the type who could adjust to this type of a complex relationship in the time to come. So he would wait for the time to decide and give a more concrete shape to the relationship between him and Aruna.

Next morning he got up with the same feeling of being able to marry Aruna sometime in future. But he realized soon that Aruna would not let it happen any day. And Alice was so sincere in her love that she would be better-off by adjusting to any kind of circumstances in order to be with Philip rather than feeling tired and giving up Philip as he had imagined the previous night.

Chapter 26

Aruna returned from her tour. She spent the whole afternoon settling down. Then towards the early evening she went around the city at her leisure. It was such a pleasure to walk around, she thought. She was comparing Paris with an Indian city at the back of her mind.

Around the historical monuments and in other hot spots for tourists she had realized that one could not escape the sight of South Asians selling bottled water, mementos, goggles, roses, roasted nuts and so on. The tangible products are mostly manufactured in China or some other low cost countries and they are sold at a throw-away price. Even for some of the perishable items like roses suppliers are at times from the developing countries. A great deal of bargaining goes on to motivate a potential buyer and the phenomenon of 'distress sale' – selling at a price with zero profit or negative profit - is not rare.

What is the background of these sellers? Aruna took a little time off trying to probe into their daily strife and she unfolded unbelievable narratives of different types.

One may tell you that he is from Punjab, paid around Rs five lakhs to the tout to travel to Italy and work in the farms. However, after the assignment is over what does he do? He might have or might not have recovered his cost. Unless he is able to incur some profit how can he return to his country? What face will he carry to his relatives? He has already sold off his farm and non-farm assets to finance his Europe tour, exploring possibilities of job opportunities. So even if he decides to return to his country what will he survive on?

He naturally travels to other countries in the common Shenzhen space where relatively better opportunities may be available or networks through national brotherhood may be operating. In the mean time his visa may have expired and his status may have been reduced to that of an illegal immigrant. However, he is able to find shared accommodation which means a medium size room with a small kitchen and a toilet with around seven to eight men of different ages huddling together to share the rent. Heating and cooling facilities are often missing, though water and electricity are available. Thanks to the Pakistani landlords who do not mind renting these accommodations to the South Asians irrespective of their religion and region of origin.

If someone is lucky enough to have the legal papers then he can go ahead and apply for Sate assistance or unemployment doll or any other support that may have been initiated. At times the country of origin also matters, it seems. As a middle aged guy selling bottled water in front of Louvre indicated, Indians have less chances of getting the State support because India is no more considered to be a developing country. The PM of India emphasized this in one of his visits, as he narrated. Bangaldeshis are in that respect better off. The State help and earnings from petty goods add up to around 350 Euros a month – 100 goes towards house rent, another hundred for living expenses and the rest remitted to the relatives back home.

Once one is inside the European space, he/she cannot go out because then there is no chance to get in again. The enormous struggle that one puts in to receive a Shenzen visa, particularly at that level of education and skill, is unforgettable. In the absence of adequate documents many a time the touts take these migrants through several illegal routes, trespassing the borders of half a dozen countries. The dream to make a fortune someday in the European land is difficult to overcome. At the same the reality bites. Thus the struggle goes on. However, what is important to note is that even within that struggling class the practice of remittances is strongly prevalent. A meager 150 Euros a month is still substantial in Indian currency to provide two full square meals a day.

Aruna thought, "How strong the family bonding is! These boys are struggling like anything yet they are so thoughtful about their relatives back home. Literally cutting their own meals they are trying to generate savings so that their starving relatives can be helped. India is great!"

"If such feelings could have been there across nations - why go that far - at least across different socio-economic classes within a country, things would have been magically different", she told herself. "But then who bothers about gross inequality which means below subsistence level of consumption for millions. People spend money of imaginary magnitude on their children's wedding but none of them talks about initiating a project at the individual level to impart skill or provide support to the poor. After donating a one rupee coin to a needy, one feels so self-satisfied!"

Two Bangladeshi boys actually begged of Aruna to pray for them. She asked them the reason of their plight. "Europe in dream is very different from actuality", they explained. Aruna smiled and murmured, "In addition if they could only understand the present crisis that the economy is going through!"

Aruna felt pathetic about some of the elderly who had migrated from the Central Asia and other East European countries. One old lady she saw was constantly on her knee begging small change. And there were so many like her. Some of the younger ones including the boys had taken to prostitution. The other day she overheard the conversation between a teenager and a middle aged man in the gardens. The boy was only seeking a few Euros possibly to buy dinner and in return he was willing to offer sexual services.

Chapter 27

Dimitri went on a tour to India. William collected a lot of tips from Aruna for him and urged him to behave himself in a foreign land. Dimitri appeared to be an easy-go type but actually he was quite a serious guy. This Aruna had realized the day she had an intensive discussion with him on feminist movement in India.

Dimitri wanted to visit Khajuraho and Konark but Aruna had already supplied a long list of temples. After spending a few days seeing the temples he was exhausted and went to Mumbai. He spent a couple of days in Bangalore as well. The attitude of the common Indians – people coming running to him to offer help – was something which impressed him a lot. He made friends with three Indian males working in multinational companies. Another guy he met through internet was employed in a call-centre and it seemed his meetings with him were more frequent as long as he stayed in Bangalore.

Both visited Mysore on a week-end and had a great deal of close interactions. Dimitri seemed to have formed a great opinion about the Indian partners, which he narrated to William in a couple of e-mails. William missed him and possibly felt a bit jealous to read those mails.

Dimitri went to the north to see the Ganges. He did not like Haridwar as it was too crowded. However, he liked Hrishikesh. The quiet atmosphere along the Ganges kept attracting him and he would often go out of his room to the river even in the depth of the night. He came across a yoga centre and took a couple of lessons. He was possibly expecting the demonstration of a couple of poses which could be used in sex. But no explicit mention of that made him a bit frustrated. He rather preferred to buy a copy of Kamasutra.

Dimitri within that short and hectic visit did learn a great deal of the Indian society and customs. He lived with a family in Gurgaon and their young daughter was his Hindi coach. Dimtri had a tremendous power of grasping things fast. He was full of admiration for the Indian family system which in his western eyes appeared highly stable and strong. He was not too bothered about the fragility that was appearing in some part of the society. That, he thought, was inevitable and insignificant. What a large percentage follows, according to him, constitutes the actual picture of a nation.

He also met with an accident, minor though. His hosts were too kind to him. The old lady in the household would not leave him alone for a minute. She massaged oil on his heel until the pain subsided and he was fit to walk around.

Dimitri was of Russian origin but had lived in France since his birth. He was good in both French and Russian. His English was rather tolerable unless he spoke on a serious issue. He started teaching French to an undergraduate in the neighbourhood. The guy offered him some money per session. But Dimitri was possibly more interested in non-monetary remunerations. The boy took the hint and was more than keen to supply it though he was already going steady with a girl in his class. Both the boy and his girlfriend seemed to have promised to each other for marriage. Dimitri felt guilty when he saw the picture of the girl in the guy's purse. But by then both had already entered into close contacts. There was no guilt feeling in the mind of the guy, though. Experimentation is the buzz-word of the day and it seems to have impacted the younger generation in a big way. Besides, Dimitri's seductive appearance must have acted as a bonus to the changing mindset.

He did not understand much about Indian spiritualism. But he started reading the Speaking Tree section in the Times of India, as long as he stayed in India. He wrote to

William in one of his mails about the depth and knowledge he had gathered from these pieces. In fact, he urged William to read them on regular basis if he could access the e-paper from Paris. He felt, William would benefit more if he read them because according to him, William had greater depth.

He bought several stuff from the state emporia in Delhi. He was greatly impressed by the wide variety of handicrafts and silk. "Why India has been exporting only low value products to Europe?" He asked the guy he taught French in the neighbourhood. "If there can be a company to manufacture readymade garments made of silk, for both males and females, they will certainly sell well in the European market. Yes, the saris and other typical Indian stuff are bought largely by the

NRIs abroad. All that cannot find a large acceptance among the Europeans except for some occasional wear. And before some multinational company comes forward to manufacture western outfits from the wide variety of Indian silk some of the Indians must try it out. Otherwise the benefits will go to the foreign companies", he explained to the guy. His student liked the idea and proposed jokingly if both of them could enter into a trading relationship.

"Yes, why not? I would explore the financial possibilities in the bank I work for", returned Dimitri with a smile. "You and I then can have innumerable trips to Europe and India, respectively."

"Another negative comment that I have to offer on India is the use and abuse of plastic", he continued. "Look at the streets, the riverbeds, the gardens, everywhere there is plastic and it is so irritating to see this non-biodegradable waste! People must understand that like soul in Indian philosophy plastic is indestructible".

The guy put his head down in shame and guilt. He too belonged to that component of the society which in spite of education behaves mindlessly. Dimitri noticed it and tried to lighten the situation. "Let's have some fun. The discussion is turning too serious, I guess", he reiterated winking at the guy. The latter smiled innocently and moved close to Dimitri.

Chapter 28

William had promised to Aruna that he would make up his mind and would let her know about his decision. He knew, Aruna was back from India but did not want to meet her until he had reached a conclusion. He thought of taking some time off and went to the south of France. He visited Cannes and spent the whole day in the beach. "The Mediterranean coast is wonderful", he thought. "What a relief from the continued winter in Paris!" Here the moderate climate has contributed to the growth of vegetation splendidly. The tall palm trees, the blue ocean and the sky and the pleasantness in the face of the human beings all add up to a heaven, William kept thinking. His mind refused to be indoors and he kept staring at the sea. The next day he spent mostly at Nice Ville. He boarded a toy train which took him around the town through its narrow lanes, across the fountains and large yellow, orange and reddish buildings with widely opened windows without grills and with a wooden frame painted in deep-green. The combination of the colours looked gorgeous. As the train climbed up the hill William's joy knew no bound. He could see the coast line, patches of structures comprising buildings of various shapes and monuments and hills nearby. The combination of rock and water is rare and that is why it looks so beautiful. The next day he went to Eze village and was more thrilled than he had expected to be. He felt as if his mind had traveled to a completely different world. A sense of composedness prevailed in him – as if he had been meditating day and night.

He had hired a room just near the beach. On his return from the Eze village when he got down at the bus station he decided to take a walk through the park. As he was coming to the end of the park and was about to step into the road again after covering the green space he came across quite a unique scene. A young lady was sitting on the cemented edge and two young boys just behind her were engaged in kissing each other. Both were in shorts. One was sitting on the floor with his legs stretched out and the other was resting on his lap with a lip-lock. There was hardly anyone on this side of the park which had given them enough privacy. However, as William reached out to the road he could find many pedestrians and vehicles moving around. William realized that the young lady was actually guarding those two boys and was cautioning them if anyone came near the staircase or was about to enter the park. Since William had come from behind he had escaped her attention. From the road the girl was visible and on the background the back of the head of only one of the two boys, just a little above the waist of the girl, could be seen. As some elderly people crossed the road and were about to reach the staircase to the park the girl whispered and the two boys separated slightly. But soon they returned to their comfort zone as none bothered to look at them.

William with great interest kept gazing at them from a distance in such a manner that he did not catch the sight of the young lady. He was quite amazed. He had already seen and done such love scenes in the streets of Paris in certain joints several times. But this time he was quite shocked. "What a great friend these two boys have in this young lady! Guarding them through and through and allowing them to enjoy when she herself is reading a book, keeping herself completely out of the act. Unique indeed!" William thought.

William entered his chamber along the coast. Evening was approaching. The sea and the sky were drawing darkness little by little. He was standing at the centre of the room. The window was wide-opened, allowing the breeze and the music of the waves to enter the room and his mind as intensely as possible.

He kept staring outside - sometimes at the sea about to hide in the depth of darkness and sometimes towards the sky lighting up the lamps one after another. "In a little while the whole starry breast of the sky would hang like a dazzling veil over the sea and it will be visible again in a new form, though", William told himself. Often we think that things do not exist as we cannot see them but in due course they come into sight maybe in a slightly different form.

He felt as if his mind was traveling to various states one above another, detaching himself from the material world. What a deliberation! Right at that moment he suddenly felt a tremendous excitement – those two love-making boys appeared before his eyes and there was disturbance between his legs. With a tremendous jerk he felt an erection. His entire body was shaking. He could count the palpitation of his heart. Blood was flowing to his penis at a rapid pace. His erection subsided as he paid attention to the blood flow in his body. But within seconds he felt its reassured presence again. It started troubling him. He could not resist anymore. Dimitri was there in every corner of his mind – pressing every cell of his physical existence. He masturbated to relieve himself. "What a unique change", he thought. Just a few minutes back he was in deep contemplation and within such a short span he was seeking an outlet. The wide space that the mind can cover within seconds kept surprising him. He slowly sat down on a chair pulling it to the window-side. His mind was completely relaxed. As if a storm had passed by! The waves from the sea were singing continuously. He unknowingly became engrossed in nature's music.

Dimitri had not disappeared from his mind. He was there in a subtle form. William pulled out the cell from his pant pocket lying on the floor and called Dimitri. He answered within seconds and on hearing his voice William felt again a hard-on. He must have Dimitri by his side at the earliest, that was the inner call of his mind. He urged Dimitri to join him in Nice. Dimitri agreed and he was in the seventh heaven. The very thought that Dimitri would join him made him excited and he was ready for another round of orgasm. He gave mild strokes to his erected penis, touched gently his own chest, legs and arms. His naked body was resting in the chair. He kepting playing with his instrument for a while, and then masturbated for the second time. This time he took longer to come but the intensity of thrill was greater. Dimitri, the two young love-making boys in the park and also a couple of other faces appeared before him while releasing himself. Then he had fallen asleep in the chair itself, resting his legs on the cot until the dawn set in and the seagulls kept screaming to grab a mouthful catch.

The morning appeared before him like a golden maid. He kept watching the rising sun, the birds whirling around the water and then chasing each other and the Eze village at a distance on the hill-top. At this point Aruna appeared before his inner eyes holding the beauty of the eastern sky. In her, he felt, the distant hill, the golden sky and the sea, all converging. William imagined as if Aruna's long black hair like the clouds on the western sky had spread over his chest. He held the pillow in both his hands: as if Aruna and he were embracing each other's existence in totality. He wanted to have her with him to enjoy this inexplicable beauty. If she were there he could have visited the Eze village with her and watched the sea from the top of the hill. The roses hanging over the head there in the palace were extraordinarily red. If Aruna were there she could have compared them with William's lips. He was eager to call Aruna but the next moment he realized that she might not have returned from India. Besides, he had already asked Dimitri to join him.

What a different situation for him! On the one hand he felt Aruna was attracting him and on the other Dimitri. "Dimitri's kisses are unforgettable and Aruna's steady beauty is imperious", he thought. On the one hand passion and on the other solemnity in each of the two relationships tore him into pieces. He wanted to escape but both were equally significant. He was astonished to observe that both the individuals were part of his nature. Both coexisted. Only the domination of one over the other kept changing from time to time. So it was an illusion for him to think that he would be able to forget one and pursue with the other. No, he needed both. But was that possible? He had promised to Aruna that he would make up his mind and would let her know who he wanted to spend his life with. Basically he was thinking to choose one between the two. What his basic self looked for was the question for which an answer he came to seek for. But at Nice he discovered that both dwelt in him: he could not eliminate any one between the two. In case he could, that was only temporary. Again the desire and longing would arise, he realized. And that would keep bothering him, spoiling his present. He would be unhappy and so also his partner if he were to choose one between the two. His unhappiness would certainly have spill-over effects. And if the partner would come to know that there remained a craze for a third person, there would be chaos indeed. "But does it happen with all other men?" thought William. Then he decided not to bother about others and their decisions. He had an issue and he must try to resolve it. If he would tell both Aruna and Dimitri about his preferences and urge them to have a better understanding of his situation they might consider, he consoled himself. He must reveal to them how desire and serenity both could be present in one. Then he kept imagining when Aruna would dominate his existence, he would pursue accordingly and then if Dimtri would take over, he would follow him sincerely. "Human being is made of both: none can have only one", he kept preaching himself.

Dimitri arrived within two days after canceling all his other assignments. William had gone to the station to receive him. They hugged each other and then William picked up his luggage. They both walked down from the station to the hotel – just a ten minutes walk. Dimitri was amazed to see the Mediterranean bay touching the shore of the Nice Ville. The landscape kept him engrossed for a while. It was still not lunch time. They decided to move on to the beach and enjoy a swim. Both quickly changed to their swim-suits and wore a towel over while crossing the street. They spent the whole afternoon at the beach consuming a couple of drinks and burgers in one of those beach-restaurants.

William had erection a couple of times while in close contact with Dimitri. Even when both just looked at each other, passion crossed his mind and he had to literally resist himself. After the evening drew in they walked back to the hotel. It was such a wonderful day, both thought. They finished their dinner in the restaurant downstairs. As soon as both entered the room Dimitri was completely spell-bound to witness the confluence of the sea and the sky in the grey twilight. Both stood near the window for a while and then grabbed each other. The current of passion in them was much stronger than in the sea. William would not let Dimitri breathe with the intensity of his mouth-kisses and Dimitri would not leave any part of William's body untouched.

After making passionate love William then stood up holding Dimitri's hips right in front of his instrument. He was giving mild strokes and caressing Dimitri's hair and breast. Dimitri was enjoying every bit of it. He was trying to extend his hands backwards in an attempt to pull William closer to his butt. William thought, just two days back he was completely lost in meditation that nature had drawn him into and then within such a short span he was enjoying so much of the physical love with Dimitri. Life is strange, he thought.

Mind cannot be discovered in whole. More you know, the more you realize that the less you know of it.

Both had fallen asleep on the floor itself till the morning breeze woke them up. They kissed each other aggressively before rushing out for a walk along the marine coast. Dimitri observed at a distance the nose of the hill piercing into the sea. William was feeling so relaxed: as if a heavy load that he was carrying on his shoulders had disappeared completely. They settled down at a spot spreading their legs to touch the water. In spite of the crowd in the beach William kissed Dimitri a couple of times while Dimitri lied relaxed in his lap. Both swam together and exchanged mouth-kisses in the water before they returned to the hotel for breakfast.

Chapter 29

Both of them returned to Paris together after spending a couple of days in Nice. William had realised by then that Dimitri was a part of this existence. Dimithri had many other associations which William knew very well. But that did not affect him much. He understood that he himself was not able to give company to Dimitri sufficiently and thus Dimitri had cultivated others. Had he decided to spend his life with Dimitri he would have been more than happy to live with him forgetting all his other affairs and associations. The lack of one led him to many; he could not be blamed, William thought.

But when William entered his studio he was again swept by the flooding memory of Aruna. The dream of a sweet home where

254

Aruna and he would share every moment of their conjugal life kept attracting him more than his passion that motivated him to invite Dimitri to join him at Nice. He called Aruna the next day and prepared himself quite well to deliver about his mental state, his on-going associations with Dimitri and his feelings for Aruna.

Happy, indeed, Aruna would be to hear about his love for her. But would she be able to accept his intense associations with Dimitri? After hearing the episodes at Nice would she at all like to see his face again? "To a western lady such narrations do not come as a surprise", William knew. "Whether Aruna can absorb them is a different issue because for Aruna such a possibility must be almost non-existent", he reflected. Of course Aruna had

had glimpses of his relationship with Dimitri. She had seen both in lip-locks. But that was a different thing. Now that they had enjoyed every moment of their meeting so intensely and had not hesitated to manifest their feelings in any manner at the physical level might be unbearable to Aruna, he wondered. William had asked for time to make up his mind, contemplating upon his preferences deeply. But he had gone one-step ahead by giving his desires a tangible shape in a more profound manner than what he had ever tried before and, more importantly, he was going to confess all of that to Aruna. Aruna's natural response, William imagined, would be to suggest him to spend the rest of his life with Dimitri. At least she would have nothing to do with William. Things went above his head.

Thoughts came upon him like a series of waves, shaking him from all angles. Yet, he stood straight. He had taken an appointment with Aruna the next day and he must come up to her upright. He should not hide anything from her and at the same time he would be honest enough to say that he would also like to be with her. Aruna might appreciate it, he thought hopefully. Notwithstanding his weakness for Dimitri he preferred to have Aruna, was no less a compliment to her. As he imagined Aruna's joy, he too felt relaxed and did not realize when he took respite in deep sleep until he got up the next morning when the door-bell rang with the arrival of the cleaner. William was waiting eagerly for the evening to arrive. He took the metro and reached the restaurant near the Saint Michael much before the time of appointment. Aruna arrived a little late. She expressed her apologies. The metro she was planning to take was delayed by a few minutes as there was a theft. William with a broad smile welcomed Aruna. Both settled down in the corner where William had already occupied the table with space for only two. William was preparing himself thoroughly to begin the conversation. At once his eyes fell on the Indian waiter and he became a little nervous, for an unknown reason. He felt he was being attracted by the Indian guy. His eyes and eye-brows were charming. He looked at Aruna, she too held so much grace. He again realized, both were casting a spell on him; two were of different types but they lead to the same path. Both the paths are so different and so common yet.

Anyway he did not have much time to churn out the commonalities or discern the differences. He started making efforts to collect himself and focus on the conversation that both had planned for.

"Aruna, it has been a great pleasure knowing you. And I have been preparing myself to propose to you. I took a bit of time to examine my weaknesses for Dimitri, which you know of. I spent a great deal of time in deep contemplation and I have made much efforts to understand myself. Now, it seems Dimitri is indispensable. If I avoid Dimitri, there will be another. So it is quite clear, even after offering myself to you sincerely there will always remain a vacuum. And how long I will be successful in withstanding and maintaining that vaccum is quite uncertain. There can be moments when that vacuum can become so much intolerable that I may do something that may shock you."

Aruna became grave. Then she smiled and said, "Well you do not have to propose to me. You can keep leading your free life the way you have been spending."

"No, that is precisely the point. I do not think I can have complete happiness with Dimitri - whether it is one Dimitri or hundreds of Dimitri. There will still be a vacuum even after getting Dimitri forever. And that vacuum will keep burning my heart for ever and ever. And you are the only respite for me from that point of view".

Aruna listened to William patiently. She could not pretend to herself anymore of not following what William has been suggesting. He had made it very clear that he would like to share his life with Aruna and Dimitri both.

"Obviously", Aruna thought, "in such kind of a relationship marriage with William is not possible. Marriage can be only between two individuals not three, Aruna recalled from the legal point of view. But next moment she told herself, marriage is simplistic in approach. It cannot address the complexity of human mind and behaviour. Aruna recalled how people pursue many affairs outside the realms of marriage. Why to scandalize the institution of marriage? It has in-capabilities to deal with the complexities of human mind but then it stands on the principle of certain commitments. If those commitments are not acceptable to someone, if one feels suffocated within the confinements of that institution then it is better not to enter it. But at the same time it is equally wrong to enter it and then pursue what the institution does not allow for." If she would have been looking for someone who would give all his hundred percent to her and vice-versa without any of the two having any urge for a third person, then the matter is different. But then she could not get William, who had a special position in her heart. The essence of spring was concealed in William. Why should she suppress her desire? At the same time to make a commitment to accept something which was not or could not be bound by the legal commitments was not all that easy. Aruna begged for time before dispersing.

But William noticed quite clearly that she did

not look disheartened, or depressed. She wanted a little more time to make up her mind. But that was alright. It was not possible for a person to accept something with a commitment without thinking about the pros and cons of the commitment that one is going to make. Any decision at haste is unstable and unsteady, thought William. Let Aruna take her time and slowly let her make up her mind. William must wait if he wanted Aruna too to have a fair share in liberty and free thinking. Aruna took long walks in the park opposite City University. She met Peter a friend of Philip. Aruna wanted to know if Philip was going steady with Alice. She asked a couple of questions to Peter before she could arrive to the main point. Of course, Aruna knew that both of them had been to the outskirts and had night stay. Peter informed directly that he had seen Philip with Alice in a restaurant near the Indian temple. Aruna thought for a moment, "Perhaps they are getting closer to each other". But the next moment she corrected herself, "Philip is such an introvert that for him spending two hours - or for that reason even two nights - with someone may actually mean nothing". She must visit Philip and find out herself what was going on.

Chapter 30

Without giving a call Aruna straight away went to the Indian temple. She was sure that she would be able to meet Philip. And she was right: Philip was there in the meditation hall and Alice was decorating the flower vase.

A little later when Philip came out of the hall Aruna and he talked a lot.

"There might have been many exceptions to Freud's view suggesting, the nicest person has the nastiest thought", started Philip.

Aruna quickly added, "However, one premise that still remains debatable is concerning nicety and self-control. Nicety is not sufficient to have self-control. And when we do not have self-control there is a nagging frustration in our sub-conscious mind which in turn prompts us to designate others as indecent creatures. This is an easy mechanism of deriving self-satisfaction because by reducing the height of the person next to us we naturally look taller. But fortunately the law of nature is very just and impartial: sooner or later the truth comes out."

After a pause Philip again came back to his point, "The evil never dies: it is as intrinsic as the good is. The twin co-exists in us. It is the constant introspection and self-analysis that keeps us vigilant over our thought process and helps us have control over the mind. The left toe of the Goddess *Durga* presses down the *asura*: an imagery representing conscience over-powering the evil in us. Anytime the evil can arise - it cannot be killed, it can only be made subservient to our conscience".

Aruna was listening attentively. She looked at the sky through the window and said, "The conscience is there in all of us. How loudly it speaks or to what extent we are able to accept its command is a critical question. Religion, by making us God-fearing, tries to maintain coherence and stability. This is definitely necessary in the initial stages. It enables us to analyse and understand. And through understanding we mature to experience realization. If realization does not come the knowledge that we acquire is useless. It remains only as a theoretical knowledge which without practice is futile. As Ramakrishna says, one has to go beneath the ocean to find gems. Movements on the surface yield nothing. With a good memory one may remember all the scriptures but without applications all that is meaningless".

Philip posed a question and then went on answering himself, "For self-analysis what is most essential? Truthfulness to the self. One has to constantly remind oneself that s(he) is not spelling it out in front of a second person. So ego should not be an issue. 'At least to myself let me be truthful' must be the *mantra*. And once one practices this sincerely one is able to take a big step towards perfection. On the other hand, by believing that we have been perfect we only welcome ignorance to dominate us. Justifying a wrong action to the self is perhaps the biggest crime on earth. On the other hand repentance, as every religion preaches, is the greatest tool for correcting one's wrong action".

Aruna smiled agreeably, "After all we have

only one life at our disposal. Why not take the fullest advantage of it and realize peace in us and bestow it on others around us? The inability to pursue self-analysis makes one adamant and self-justifying. And on failing to convince everybody the person becomes vindictive. But all this is suicidal. It kills the self little by little, unknowingly. And one day the person realizes that s(he) has been reduced to a liability. Then begins the action to form groups of likeminded people - some vague attempts in search of satisfaction, realizing little that it has disappeared from the inner chambers long ago."

Philip recollected his teachings from the spiritual centre, "Saints usually recommend productive activity to keep the mind constantly engaged and to avoid negative thoughts. To do a crime and to think to do a crime are equally harmful to the self. Creative activities, meditation and service to the destitute help one to empty the vessel so that it can hold newer things. Else the old will keep bothering us".

Aruna quickly added, "No action is perfect in absolute sense: as smoke surrounds fire, every action will also have loop wholes in some sense or the other (*Gita*). So withdrawal from *karma,* fearing criticism is not the solution. The role of conscience in this context is indeed important in determining action that will generate greater positive impact and minimize social evil. If we are conscious of this fact, a much better world can definitely emerge as with this motivation there will be less space for conflict. The scientific discoveries will contribute to social harmony and complementary relationships will exist among various stake holders. With greater possibility of convergence among all an efficient system will emerge to ensure greater welfare. Human mind will acquire the ability to rise above the dogma and will begin to wonder, from which will emerge the philosophy, newer thoughts and paradigms".

Philip was growing impatient to know if Aruna was going to be with him not just as a friend but much more than that which includes a romantic and an intellectual association. After a couple of pleasantries he asked her directly. She almost said explicitly that she would like to be with him forever but at the same time she wanted to know the developments that had taken place between him and Alice. Aruna was happy on the one hand to imagine that her efforts to put Alice and Philip together had not gone in vain. On the other hand, she was a bit lost to think that Philip might not be hers only. What a unique feeling! The same phenomenon which gives joy from one side can be disturbing from another. But then that is how life is!

On Aruna's response Philip felt as if someone provided a practical shape to what was embedded in him, what was lying in his dream world. He quickly kissed her, "I have been dying to hear this, Aruna," he said. Both were in the garden. The tender sun-light could not bring much warmth but definitely visibility. And sometimes clear visibility is so important in life!

Alice could see both of them from the

window. She had the decency not to follow them when Aruna offered to talk to Philip. Alice stood near the window for a while. Her hands were still engaged in cleaning the flowers she wanted to put in the vase. Unknowingly she had spent a lot of time gazing at the two in the garden and that is when Aruna caught her sight. Aruna asked Philip bluntly to make sure that both Philip and Alice had been comfortable with each other, "What are you thinking about Alice?" Philip did not know what to say. Aruna went ahead without waiting to receive any response from him. "No, no Philip. I have told you in the past. I cannot see you leaving Alice. Her feelings for you are so pure and sincere. Don't ask her to stay away from us. Why can't she have the right to be with you? If two people can be happy being together, why not three? Why does she have to be left alone? Why does she have to find another person to be happy? Don't we have enough space between us to accommodate sincerity? She too deserves to be with you".

Philip didn't know what to say. He at last nodded his head, unmindfully though. He was not really able to grasp what Aruna was saying though he himself had already given a lot of assurances to Alice. To commit verbally and then to implement it are two different things. Perhaps he was then feeling the burden of his commitment. After all relationship is not friendship, he thought! Aruna could read it in his eyes. "Why not Philip? If we two are in a relationship it does not mean that we are together for all seven days in a week and all twenty-four hours in a day. You think about so many things other than me. And so do I. You meet so many people and so do I. Why does then the problem arise when you think about someone other than me on a romantic plane? You being serious with someone does not reduce in any manner the seriousness of your relationship with me. I am fine with the idea that someone else is in your life. Can't you love two persons simultaneously? That is a different matter that our selfishness does not want to share the space with someone else. But that possessiveness comes from insecurity. Once you remove that insecurity I don't think there is any problem in sharing. Insecurity comes from excludability. Yours and my relationship does not involve excludability. In case it does it is only momentarily like now I am talking to you certain things in which Alice may not like to participate".

"Aren't you legitimizing polygamy?" Asked Philip quite bluntly with a big laugh.

Aruna looked seriously into his eyes and then replied, "No, Philip, I am not. Let me repeat. I am talking about the possibility of sharing something with more than one individual. Yes, you may criticize that 'someone' and something have suddenly become the same. But let me tell you very frankly, there is not much difference between an individual and an object. Your attitude is more important. If it is there for a 'thing' it can be there for a 'person' as well. Possessiveness requires no excuse. Don't you know how much bloodshed people can have over a piece of land even after having enough for themselves to reside? Aruna posed for a while, "And, Philip, when I plead for sharing don't you think I am not being stingy to myself either? I am also assigning enough space to myself. I don't promise to be thinking about only you all the while. I can also love someone as much as I love you and may like to be with him as well. Look, let me take this opportunity to tell you that William is in my life. Yet, I have thought so much about you that I cannot express in words. More I think to choose one between the two, more difficult it becomes. So, I have decided to accept what comes to me spontaneously. I don't want to force myself into something that someone else thought to be ideal. For me idealism is something that my mind accepts and believes in. I wish to be in relationship with you and William both because I have intense feelings for both of you. Is that acceptable to you Philip?"

Aruna was not expecting any reply from Philip. She was only making a declaration. She knew that it would not be as easy for Philip as it was for her. The offer of two to Philip himself was more acceptable to him than the possibility of two for Aruna. It is not a question of male or female. It is the question of the self. The self wants a bigger choice set and if it comes unasked for, why should not one be happy. But if it goes to someone else there can be heart-burning, question of risk and instability. Pragmatism lies in the ability to see others as the 'self'. Aruna did not want to read the expressions of Philip either. She thought, he must have time to absorb and assimilate. Aruna bade good-bye and took leave of him. She went inside the temple to say bye to Alice. Alice was not too comfortable to see Aruna, though she tried her best to be very pleasant and graceful to her.

Chapter 31

"Aruna was planning to meet William the same evening. But he was not in the town, it seemed. Even after several calls, she received no response. Aruna felt he must have gone out with Dimitri. A feeling of emptiness prevailed in her, which led to annoyance as well. The number is not important in killing seclusion. If number could solve the problems then countries with excess population would have been the best performers. She felt isolated even after having two persons being close to her. She struggled and tried to accept isolation as a part of life. It has to exist because it is important too. If there will be the company of someone always, the self cannot see itself. Besides, if you want space for yourself, you have to allow space to others and the moment you agree to deliver freedom to others you should be willing to accept isolation for yourself. Her annoyance started melting away as she reflected more on this. If she was going to walk on a path that was different from what was being largely followed, then she must be prepared for all the consequences as well. After all, it was her choice no; one had imposed it on her. If she wanted the cake, she had to take the wrapper as well. How she would manage to dispose off the wrapper was her look out. She looked through the window. The white flowers on the tree-top looked like the icing on the cake. "Life is indeed beautiful," she thought optimistically.

Aruna ultimately managed to get in touch with William. First she thought that she would get both Philip and William together to have a meeting among the three. But then why? She did not owe an explanation to anyone. It was completely her choice that she liked both. And if Philip also liked her and so did William, why did she have to make efforts to create a cordial relationship between Philip and William. They could remain strangers to each other. All she would have to do is to inform both that she had taken both seriously. And that she had already done as far as Philip was concerned. William perhaps had to be told more explicitly if she already had not. But it should not be very difficult for William to accept, she thought.

She met William over a cup of coffee. The evening breeze was blowing over the city and Aruna was enjoying her coffee. She slowly unfolded her story.

"William, I might have told you or not I don't remember exactly. But let me be very clear on a particular point that I have both you and Philip in my life. And I don't believe in choosing one between the two. If both have appealed to me then be that so. I don't want to bring in any social or ethical considerations here. Now, please don't think that I am asking for your permission either. I am only informing you as I have informed Philip. Like you appreciate Dimitri's company and mine both I too want to be with you as well as Philip. If that is a problem for you let me know very explicitly. For me acceptance does not have to be accompanied by rejection. Often in this world people have to pick up something and reject something else. Why can't we endorse everything that has come in our way and particularly so, if we have liked all of that. Space is not a problem, William. Human mind has lot of it. All you need is to convince yourself to accept what you believe in. Our difficulty arises because what we believe in may not be in coherence with what many others accept. But why do we have to bother about what others like or dislike as long as we do not cause any harm to them. Many may not appreciate this logic and our way of life and thinking because they have not learnt to understand their mind and giving preference to their inner feelings. They have been either scared or the mindset of the neighbourhood has been so overbearing that they rarely get an opportunity to hear their inner voice".

Aruna had talked a lot at a stretch. She

stopped and took a sip from her cup. William kept gazing at her. He smiled and said, "Yes let us not bother too much about 'many others' and how they will accept our relationship".

"Let us contemplate upon the stability of our multiple relationships. I don't bother too much about the long run. At the moment if it works it is fine."

"True, Aruna that is what I want. As long as it works it is fine. Nobody wants to carry a carcass on the shoulder."

Aruna passed a sigh of relief. They both hugged each other for a while before they could depart.

Chapter 32

Aruna received a detailed letter from her mother. Her mother could not use the internet and so had to adopt the old-fashioned method to communicate. Aruna read the letter carefully. She had blamed Aruna a lot for not having married Amit. Baby managed to develop intimacy with Amit and most probably they were going to be married in the next few months, she wrote. She always thought that Amit and Aruna would make a very good match. But all in vain! Aruna had her own ways. She was always adamant and never paid any heed to her good advice. The time would come when she would certainly realize her mistake but by then it would be too late, she had forecasted.

Aruna was getting tired of reading the letter.

But, she knew her mother was her greatest well-wisher. The only problem was that she judged good and bad from her point of view. However, it was also very natural for her not to accept what Aruna thought to be right. Her background and her lack of exposure to the outside world were strong determinants of her perception and views. Aruna remembered the points quite well.

Then the letter moved on to describe the neighbourhood issues. Indu had left her husband to marry an American. Sumanta was quite upset about the whole thing. What ever domestic issues they had, had actually become prominent in the public domain. People were worried about their daughter. It seemed both fought over the custody of the girl and then it had moved to the court for settlement.

Bilas and his wife did not get along and one day both had a major quarrel, inviting public intervention in a significant way. His daughter would be very cunning when she would grow up and so on.

Aruna reflected on the contents, "People talk about marriage all the while but does it have any stability when it comes to good feelings for each other? No doubt, marriage is the greatest institution in the world. And just because she herself did not pursue it, its value must not be discounted at an unreasonable rate. There must have been a number of advantages or else it would not have survived through centuries. However, if it is not able to render stability at the mental plane then why is has to continue. The alternates are no better – rather more fragile - but then they do not have any false image or make false promises to yield ethereal bliss. They have their doors of entry and exit wide open. Expectations are nominal and so also the duties and responsibilities. It is only trust and feelings on the basis of which life goes on. No one has to carry a cadaver on the shoulder in the name of duty."

Aruna's progressive views kept glittering before her eyes. She was not going to preach her views to the rest of the world. What she had thought good for herself she pursued and as long as she could be happy it was absolutely fine. Of course her friends, relatives and well-wishers who judge things from their own point of view would not be able to appreciate what she followed. But that was okay. There might be new types of uncertainties including health risks but then marriage too could not provide a safety-jacket either. There has been plethora of incidents depicting lack of faith and love among the married individuals around the globe even if one keeps aside the minor incidents of conjugal violence, she thought.

Aruna combed her hair and got ready to go for a walk. Unfortunately she met Nina as soon as she was downstairs. Nina had come to the locality to buy some second hand and cheap stuff which she could use as "foreign gifts" in her forthcoming visit to India. All that was more than enough for her bunch of starving relatives back India. They could not deserve anything better, Nina always thought.

She was wearing a gorgeous Indian suit, not matching her personality. A couple of bags hanging from her both the shoulders and a few in her hands. Aruna suddenly recalled that Nna's husband had committed suicide. Not an ounce of sadness she could see in her face, though. However, Aruna could not avoid the minimum decency. She thought, she must stop and greet Nina before she moved on.

As soon as Nina saw Aruna, she turned away her face as a first reaction. But then when Aruna approached her and expressed her condolences on her husband's untimely passing away, she thought of responding. After nodding her head as a mark of accepting the empathy she quickly asked her, "So when are you going to be married to Philip? But then someone in the Indian temple said, you are in love with another guy as well. So you are planning to have two husbands? Well done, Indian girl! A Modern Draupadi!"

Aruna could not say anything in embarrassment. Nina took the advantage and went on, "Which court of law will you use to legitimize your marriage?"

Aruna decided to leave without uttering a single word. But Nina then served an unsolicited and thunderous prediction, "Who knows that these men do not have innumerable partners? A store house of HIV-AIDS! You nasty girl, defaming the country!"

For a moment Aruna thought, she would return the pleasantries generously! And she did have a lot to offer on marriage and husband-wife relationship. But she controlled herself and moved away fast.

She did not want to think about the

unpleasantness that had just occurred. However, notwithstanding her anger she realized that she would have to get prepared for more such harsh comments. There could be situations and people from whom she would not be able to run away as she did a little while ago. She would have to keep her arguments ready. And she would have to explain them gently. Else, who was going to buy her theory? She might not have to care for that but at the same time she must not keep quiet like a fool, her conscience dictated.

Chapter 33

Several months had passed. Aruna and Philip were returning from Chamonix, Mont Blanc. They spent almost two weeks holidaying in the mountains. The French Alps looked wonderful and so was their love life. Aruna was cheerful and Philip was in the seventh heaven. At the station Philip asked her to accompany him to his residence. But she refused because she had to prepare her seminar paper which was scheduled for the following week. Aruna got innumerable innovative ideas when she was romancing with Philip. Lying down half on Philip's chest she kept watching the Alps and thinking about the contents of her paper. She promised to be with him again after a month because after the seminar she would have to spend sometime with William as well. He had been insisting her to go with him to Germany. His relatives were in Frankfort. He must meet them with Aruna. Let them see the new addition to their family.

William was supposed to come to the station in case he had returned from Greece. Aruna looked around – no he was not there anywhere. So he was still having gala time with Dimitri in Greece! Aruna sent a quick SMS to Dimitri, "You seem to be squeezing him a lot". Aruna received a reply immediately, "Saved enough for you". "Naughty fellow", Aruna smirked. The next moment she got a call from William informing her that they would return to Paris after two more days. He would not disturb Aruna till her seminar was over. But after that he would seek tons of love and it was completely Aruna's responsibility to make his holidays fruitful. Aruna agreed smilingly.

Alice had been waiting for Philip eagerly. Now he had the responsibility to give her company. Philip was pleasantly surprised to see that she had adjusted to this complex relationship quite smoothly. She had no complaints nor she felt neglected when he was away with Aruna. Philip pursued his spiritual journey simultaneously. Whenever he had time he kept visiting the Indian temple and its spiritual centre.

Aruna had said goodbye to Philip and boarded the metro. She kept thinking about their romantic moments in the hotel. "Both Philip and William are so different!" she thought. "Both have their unique ways of initiating and pursuing romance. Both are different, yet the moments spent with both are enjoyable and fulfilling. Definitely no overlap", she confirmed to herself. The yogic positions in sex with Philip were incomparable. She looked forward to her trip with William. "William's cute red lips are too hot! His fingers are always desperately hovering around to grab. Oh to be with him is like moving in a roller-coaster!" she remarked to herself.

Life went on. William was the most enjoyable partner of Dimitri, Aruna recalled of having heard from Dimitri himself. Yet, there was no issue when she and William were together. Dimitri dropped in a number of times when William was with Aruna but without any hesitation he provided them space and opportunities. If Aruna had learnt anything from Dimitri it was this that by becoming possessive one could never be happy. She had organized herself to offer opportunities gracefully to William and Dimiri even if he ever came at the wrong moments.

In her leisure hours she kept reflecting on issues that she and Philip discussed. The role of conscience in the context of material life and experiencing the changelessness in the midst of changes were some of the topics which were unforgettable. On the other hand, she recalled William would always be keen to discuss social issues including inequality and the State failures.

In one of her letters to her father Aruna wanted to convey that happiness could be found in new situations also. To have its fulfillment one does not have to follow the same path that one's predecessors have already paved or recommended to adopt. No one wants to take the risk; therefore everyone wants to follow the prescribed path. But if one can undertake risk one may find greater happiness. And undertaking risk means one has to stop following the recommended path blindly. Why should one go the stereotyped way, after all? Of course flexibility requires caution as well, for, it may expose to greater possibilities of being vulnerable. But then for the sake of safety and security one does not have to stop being innovative or imaginative. Nor one has to make compromise with happiness. Even without any legal standing the new practices can become popular. And Aruna did not see any practical issue in nurturing them. Nor did she expect Philip or William to have any issue if she understood both correctly.

The new ways are about to bloom. No body can insist on adopting the old. When few take the new path they are deviants but then when it will be followed by innumerable that will become the practice. Like everything in the world the society too is evolving. There can be moments when the changes are smooth and continuous and there can be times when the changes are discreet and kinked. If one has the audacity to float with time, there is no challenge, there is no handicap. When you keep observing and understanding the changes they cease to be fearful or misleading because the unknown component in them which actually scares you all the while becomes too familiar to you. The rules of the game are important. If one understands them well and accepts them from within, there cannot be frustration, there cannot be unhappiness. You do not have to refuse desire but you must know the rules of desire and the rules of pursuing it. Then you are unmoved by the flow even when you are actually flowing. You are not perturbed even when you are completely unaware of the future. Too much of exactness in prediction can actually harm the charm of existence. And for sure, the unknown is more charming than what you know, simply because it is unknown. That unknown is constantly emerging and evolving from what you have known. Do not hamper its growth by clinging to only what you have known. Do not worry about its limit of evolution. The stream after completing its journey meets the ocean which is endless.

ABOUT THE AUTHOR

Arup Mitra is professor of Economics, Institute of Economic Growth, Delhi. His area of research interest includes development, labour, urban, gender and industrial economics. He has published a number of books and more than one hundred research papers in various international and national journals. His recent book on inclusive growth, employment and wellbeing has been published by Springer and his co-authored book on corruption and development in the Indian economy is published by Cambridge. Besides, he writes in various business dailies. He received the Mahalanobis memorial gold medal from the Indian Econometric Society for his outstanding contribution to quantitative economics.

His activities extend beyond economics. In the field of literature he has published four volumes of poems and a fiction: Awakening (1998) by Commonwealth publishers, In Search of the Lotus-Feet (2002) by Atlantic Publishers, Light on the Lotus (2007) by Readworthy, Poverty Profile (2009) by Mind Melodies and A Letter to Mother: From Destruction to Construction (2002) by Atlantic Publishers.

He has been trained as a classical dancer in the Odissi style by Guru Dibakar Khuntia and earned Nritya Visharad from the Prachin Kala Kendra. He has performed in many important centers.

He also pursues philosophy and spiritualism and writes in the Speaking Tree section of the Times of India.